Wanted to warm you up a ver ures make you think of your days in the Carribean .

Take Care.
Capt Dav Y

The Nautilus Project

By: Capt. David S. Yglesias

DOLPHIN/CURTIS PUBLISHING

This is a work of fiction. All main characters and events portrayed in this book are fictional and any resemblance to real people or incidents is purely coincidental. However some names, locations and establishments that are made reference to are indeed factual.

David Yglesias
Copyright ©2003

Maria Yglesias
Cover Art

Ken Keidel
Editing

Armando Mato
Cover Design

Page 20 photo courtesy of Bertram Yachts.
Page 56 and back cover photos courtesy Ken Keidel

Published by Dolphin/Curtis Publishing
8033 N.W. 36 Street, Miami, FL 33166

ISBN: 0-9702677-3-8

Printed in the United States of America

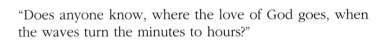

"Does anyone know, where the love of God goes, when the waves turn the minutes to hours?"

Gordon Lightfoot,
"The Wreck of the Edmund Fitzgerald," 1976.

This book is dedicated to my wonderful wife Maria, our beautiful children Laura, Eric and John, and the rest of my clan. Special thanks to my Mom and Dad and my teachers, especially Ms. Timmis, who taught me never to give up, and that imagination has no boundaries or limits. With imagination you are free to journey anywhere and everyday life can become a pure adventure.

CHAPTER ONE

The ship had arrived just after midnight, and with hopes of a quick turnaround the crew had started unloading cargo immediately after clearing customs. The Swedish captain remembered the sadistic look on the face of the Cuban security officer, Major Suarez, as he broke the seal on the shrouded manifest and removed its contents. Not knowing exactly what they had just transported halfway across the planet from Massawa, Ethiopia, made even the seasoned captain quite uncomfortable.

It was only 6:50 a.m., and already the mostly Philippine crew of the Panamanian flagged tanker Addis was drenched in sweat. With the exception of some shabby fishing vessels heading out to sea, Havana Harbor was quite serene.

The evil-looking major made him feel exceedingly more uneasy. He had an appearance he had witnessed in Eastern Europe many years earlier, the look of a fascist in search of total control, with no concern for the cost.

Below the ship, a caravan of tanker trucks formed a neat single-file. With clamorous air pumps running full bore, the white powdery payload was being efficiently pumped into the awaiting tankers. The trucks bore no markings normally required of hazardous material. What were we really carrying? wondered the captain.

As soon as a truck was loaded, a packet containing a bill of materials labeled "Fluoride" was handed to a driver. The delivery address was to one of the many water treatment facilities throughout the island.

By 10:30 a.m. the ship's hold, now empty, was sanitized and being loaded with raw cane sugar for the voyage home.

CHAPTER TWO

I t was another beautiful day in paradise. Jim Riley was sitting on his deck overlooking Florida Bay. Jim finished his third cup of coffee and put down his morning paper. Like most, he had his daily ritual, and Jim's morning routine started with the sports section and ended with the front page.

Almost hidden from view, in the lower right hand corner of the front page was a tiny excerpt from a White House correspondent. It explained how Congress had once and for all abandoned its search for unaccounted prisoners of war in Vietnam.

It was not much of an article, but Jim's mind could not help racing back to a moment nearly three decades earlier. The years had been a friend, putting distance between those insane days of covert combat missions and his now relatively normal existence.

Laws of physics, such as time and distance, reduced the occasions spent dwelling on the past, but the baggage Jim carried took on a life of its own, always popping up at inopportune instances, unannounced.

He remembered strolling down Duval Street in Key West one sweltering June day last year. A toothless street person selling handmade hats made of coconut palm leaves eagerly shoved a hat in Jim's direction. Uncontrollably, Jim's mind raced back to a muddy riverbank, where a gaunt sniper, wearing a rice patty straw hat and tattered clothes, was also missing most of his teeth. Burnt into Jim's memory was the horrid look of fear on the man's face. With Jim's K-bar knife imbedded deep in the man's sternum, the Viet Cong guerilla knew death awaited him as Jim twisted the lethal blade.

The hardest memories were of comrades, inescapably trapped or shot and dying, and ordered to be left behind. Seeing a young man in the prime of his life, losing a leg to a land mine as blood and life drained from his body. The young man's eyes not as much filled with pain but more of fear and disbelief. Leaving a man from your unit, even when they have only a handful of breaths left, was the toughest part.

The sound of a truck coming down the winding drive that led to his house snapped Jim's mind out of his sudden funk. The morning was still and quiet. With little or no breeze, the dense air was pungent with a smell of the tropics. The gumbo-limbo trees and the jasmine created a combination fragrance that no perfume could ever hope to re-create.

As an old rusty truck pulled into view, the tires made a crunching noise as they traveled down the crushed coral drive. When the Chevy pickup was almost in front of the house, Jim's 12-year-old black lab, Skipper, let out a long wailing cry. In his younger days, Skipper would have picked out Larry's truck when it turned off US 1, the Overseas Highway as locals call it. It was hard for Jim to accept that even Skipper was getting on in years. As Jim put on his Florida State University cap and looked in the mirror, he realized just how quickly life flies by.

Only a few years ago his tan face was tight and his hair

light brown. Everyone always thought Jim was at least 10 years younger than he really was. Now as he brushed his teeth, he could clearly see the crow's feet in the corners of his eyes. The gray in his hair and mustache gave him a salt and pepper look.

Was it hours of exposure to tropical sun or just working around the punishing salt water? he wondered, as he looked down into the palms of his scabrous hands. Jim would simply have to shake someone's hand to know that they, too, made their livelihood from the sea. Jim's hands and skin appeared almost leathery, not the soft-smooth buckskin kind, more like worn and defaced rawhide.

His hands may have lacked the calluses of someone swinging a pick ax from 8 to 5, but they were nonetheless intensely tough. After years of being nicked by fish hooks, pricked by marine life, burnt from screaming mono filament fishing line flying between fingers, the surface of his palms and fingers had hundreds, if not thousands, of microscopic imperfections. Almost like tiny fishing barbs, they would snag anything with which they made contact. Jim's wife Linda had ruined many a pair of panty hose to his well-intended, but destructive, wandering hands.

The ex-Navy Seal could do nothing to slow down the steady march of time, but he refused to simply give in to the constant tug of gravity. He remembered that after turning 30, everything he ate seemed to head straight for his mid-section. He could almost sense his metabolism winding down with every peanut butter cup. Trying to take the easy route, he tried all kinds of quick fixes. In the end, however, the old dreaded drudgery of diet and exercise were the only ways he achieved success. Through constant work, he remained fit as hell.

Jim had married Linda 21 years earlier. Linda was the type of person who could eat most anything and still looked great sunning on the bow of the boat. When they would go to the all you-can-eat buffet at Whale Harbor Inn, Jim would swear she could eat her own weight in Alaskan crab claws. She never gained an ounce.

It was painful for Jim to think back on the early years of their marriage. They had been best friends. They enjoyed doing everything together. As the years drifted by, they were faced with the normal challenges that couples face, but they had always pulled through. Lately, however, they had gotten off track.

Jim could not put his finger on it, but something was definitely wrong. You could just sense the distance. It took years to reach this point. They were no longer soul mates; they were now barely roommates. Too many days out on the water, old boy, not enough time in port where you belonged, thought Jim, as he gave himself a fake grin and nodded at the mirror.

Hearing footsteps on the deck outside, Jim headed for the door.

"Good Morning, Jimbo," first mate Larry said as the squeaky screen door slammed behind him.

"Fishing might be tough, but it looks like a great day on the water. Not a whisper of wind," Jim said as they both stepped onto the wooden deck outside the house.

At 6:45am it was hard to see exactly how nice it would be, but from their vantage point the bay looked like the glass of a huge tabletop. The early morning colors reflecting off the water filled the setting with panoramic hues of blues, reds and lavenders.

Larry and Jim had been friends for a long time. Larry Shea was of medium height and stocky, he had shoulder-length brown hair, tied neatly in a braided ponytail. Larry also held a captain's license, but he would never amount to anything more than an excellent first mate.

Larry had grown up fast around the shrimp docks of

Key West. He never knew his father and was raised by a mother who took to the bottle. Even so, he still had a good outlook on life and for the most part stayed out of trouble. Jim had tried to teach Larry the little things that made a successful charter boat captain in the Florida Keys, but Larry just never had the patience.

Putting up with cute girls in bikinis with no fishing ski-ills was one thing. Having to kiss some client's ass and tell him what a great job he did pulling in the "Big One" was just too difficult for him. He left the salesmanship of fish-ing to Jim. No one could ever touch Larry's skill at rigging baits and actually hooking fish. Back at the fish docks they clearly proved that. The Jim and Larry fishing machine had fast become a legend in the Florida fishing tournament circles.

For being in retirement, Jim had never worked so hard. When he first started fishing professionally, it had been just for fun. As serious anglers began to see his talents, he found himself working more and more days. During the summer, he was lucky to get one day off a week. A day off for them usually meant more work, keeping up on maintenance. It was no wonder Linda oftentimes got impatient with the lack of time they spent together.

But Linda could tell where he was heading in his last career. Propelled by his military training, Jim was far and away the youngest executive at I-Mark. Jim's competitive nature was causing him to work at a pace that could only lead to burnout.

Thank goodness for corporate takeovers! With a stock swap from his largest competitor, Jim got out when most were just getting their first promotions. Jim thrived under high pressure and at least out on the water he did not have the fax machines, the beepers and the multiple lines blinking.

Jim loved his fishing. Even after eight years, fishing never got old to him. Running a computer software company surely had. It must be the control, he thought. Out in the Gulf Stream he depended on no one, no cranky technical support people, no temperamental programmers, just Larry, himself and the ocean.

Jim and Linda lived in a typical Keys home with just a few modifications. It was built of concrete blocks up on stilts. Linda designed the floor plan herself. They could have saved money here and there, but they decided to spare no expense and build it to withstand a "Category Five" hurricane.

Category Five was not a code listed in the Monroe County Building Codes, but a special code built to survive a hurricane with sustained winds of 180 mph or more. Instead of having wooden beams in the roof, it was solid concrete. Every section of poured concrete was reinforced with steel Rebar. Windows had built in hurricane shutters, which could be closed at a moment's notice. Linda called the house "Fort Knox" both because it was built like a fort and because it cost so damn much to construct.

The best part about their property was the privacy. True privacy was hard to come by in the Keys. They had a wooded acre, hidden from view from all angles but the Florida Bay. On the water there was a dock, and by the dock stood a lone coconut palm tree. Under that solitary palm there were two wooden beach chairs, with white peeling paint, blistered from the unrelenting Florida sun.

Due to constant breezes from southeast trade winds, the palm had a distinct bow to it. Years of birds, insects and hurricanes had left its bark scarred and pock-marked. The weathered trunk reminded Jim of himself. The sound of palm leaves fluttering in the breeze was as relaxing to Jim as cool summer rain hitting a rusty tin roof.

This was one of Jim's favorite places on the planet. From here he could look out on the bay and solve most of the world's problems usually with just one ice-filled glass of 12-year-old Scotch.

CHAPTER THREE

It was just before sunrise when the wail of a newborn baby abruptly awoke a family's slumber in a tiny apartment located in the center of Cardenas, Cuba. Instinctively, the weary-eyed mother jumped to her feet, put on her robe and scrambled down the darkened hallway to a shabby room, resembling a makeshift nursery.

It was their first child and both parents were constantly exhausted from such little sleep and the rigorous demands of a newborn. Groggy and still half asleep, the loving mother could still not resist a cheerful smile, as she picked up her red-faced crying baby and held her tight against her chest.

Opening her nightgown she sat down in an old wooden rocker and offered the baby her breast. As the baby's lips made contact with the nipple, the infant instinctively began making sucking sounds. With one taste of the mother's warm milk, however, the baby abruptly backed her tiny head away and once again commenced screaming.

This was becoming a regular occurrence. Tears of frustration began to well up in the mother's eyes. Feelings of both rejection and incompetence overwhelmed her, as the baby screamed on. After several tense and unsuccessful attempts, she finally took her baby into the kitchen and gave the child the only nourishment that produced tranquility in the Sanchez home.

With baby formula unavailable, tap water was free and sugar cane plentiful. She guiltily made up a bottle of guarapo de cana and gave it to her tiny gift from God. Sucking down the bottle aggressively, the little angel smiled with satisfaction as she burped.

With her eyes glassy and trance-like, the infant began to once again fall asleep. Laying the child down and tucking her tightly into her sheets, the woman wondered, what is in that water?

CHAPTER FOUR

As an olive green Russian-built tractor and tanker pulled into the water treatment center in the town of Cardenas, Doctor Ernesto Gonzalez was already standing by, awaiting the load. Although Dr. Gonzalez specialized in the field of nuclear biophysics, he had become the island's chief scientist in conjunction with any dark project having to do with the intelligence department.

The rig made a slight squeal, then a resounding swoosh as the driver applied the parking brakes. Opening an inspection cover, Ernesto gingerly removed a sample and placed it in a vile. Entering the main office he headed to a makeshift laboratory. Adding several solvents, he was able to calculate the purity of the cargo to within 2 percent.

Within minutes he was on the phone with the chemists at the other water treatment facilities instructing them of the proper dosage to administer. For a man with very little self-esteem, it made Ernesto feel quite powerful prescribing this consequential cocktail. At his discretion he could desolve a few more kilos here and there and control an entire population.

CHAPTER FIVE

At 6:50 a.m. it was time to get down to the docks. Getting into Larry's old pickup they headed for Whale Harbor Marina. As they pulled into the parking lot, Jim looked up at the large American flag flying outside the restaurant. It lay limp, not a hint of wind.

When Jim first started in this business he would turn on the cable each morning, eager to hear what the National Weather Service would predict for the day. After a while he figured out that the people predicting the weather must be locked in a room with no windows.

If a report called for 3-foot seas it would actually be plus or minus 2 feet. Hell, he could do better than that without one look at a weather map. So the Whale Harbor flag and the horizon became his most reliable weather forecast.

As Jim got out of the truck he took in the distinct smells of the dock. It was a complicated mixture of aromas aged over the many years. There was a slight oily smell of diesel fuel, a slight stench of decaying fish; last night's spilled beer and the scent of fried sausage, bacon and eggs being served in the adjoining restaurant. If he were blind, he could have found this place from a mile away.

Walking the dock to the boat, he passed a series of photos on the walls. Old and faded by weather and time, they could easily be overlooked. For Jim, however, it gave him a sense of the history of Whale Harbor. Some of the greatest captains in modern time had at one time or another plied these waters. Most were gone now, yet some still fished on.

Jim just happened to glance at an old faded picture on the wall. It was Capt. Earl "Deuce" Sorrintino, standing by his crew and smiling with an impressive catch of king mackerel.

Deuce was one of Jim's biggest fishing heroes. Like almost everyone at Whale Harbor, Jim had mated for him early on. Some people actually do look their age. Not Deuce, for as long as Jim had known him, he always appeared old. When Jim had worked for him, Deuce looked like he should have retired 10 years earlier.

Without complaint he would hobble around, barely able to climb up his fly bridge, the cartilage in his knees having long ago been pounded into nothing but scar tissue from years of riding Gulf Stream swells.

His skin always appeared peppered with blister-like sores. He once took a dermatologist on a charter who swore that the worst patient she had ever examined had skin twice as healthy as Deuce's. He was hardheaded, though, and just never believed in sun block.

"Those damn chemicals! They'll get into your live well and before you know it you'll lose 200 pilchards in five minutes," he'd say.

Deuce was right, Jim had experienced first-hand what happens when an inexperienced mate poisons an entire hold of live bait, reaching hands in the live-well water coated with Australian Gold SPF 35.

Captain Deuce never had a bad thing to say about anybody, except for whichever mate was currently working for him. Deuce believed that mates were inherently lazy and for the most part unreliable. God knows you would not want to be mating for him and show up late, drunk or hung over.

Jim remembered one of Decue's favorite jokes. "You know what they call a mate when he breaks up with his girlfriend, don't you?"

"What?" his customer would eagerly ask.

"Homeless! That's what you'd call the lazy son of a bitch!" he would bellow with a roar of laughter.

The poor bastard who worked for Deuce truly endured the hell of his tutelage. However, when those mates finally did "punch their ticket" and receive their own captain's license, there would be no one better trained.

When your eyes met Deuce's, he would look at you with honor bestowed on only the few who actually made it through the program. Jim, like so many others, forgot just how many times he had wanted to commit treason on the high seas. Although Jim treated his mates differently, Jim really loved the guy.

It was just this past January, when prostate cancer finally tightened its slow grip on Deuce. Like a fishing reel, Deuce's passion for living was set for maximum drag, but even after a valiant battle, cancer took him deep and sounded. His rod and reel of life was spooled. When the great ones go, they go in honor and tradition in Islamorada.

Many of the captains on charter boat row got their start mating for Captain Deuce. In that way, what had been learned and proven by one man is handed down to the next. In that way you never really die, you still live on in spirit.

The Allbright Knot, the Bob Lewis Kite, they all serve their place in history. The old adage that there is nothing more important to a captain than time on the water is never so apparent as in the passing down of knowledge.

It was the culmination of this respect that provided Deuce his greatest honor. After his death, his body was cremated. Every charter boat from Key Largo to Bud N'

Mary's Marina in Islamorada called for lines out early that day and headed for "The Point," off Davis Reef.

Not much in life is truly predictable, but on most days one thing was certain: At some time during the day you would find old Deuce fishing "The Point." It was far and away his favorite place on his long list of not-so-secret spots.

As the fleet approached, they all positioned their stern toward one another. With everyone's VHF radio switched to Channel 79, anyone who wished read a eulogy over the air. Jim remembered many incredible things that were said on that calm winter day. But it was Capt. Skip Bradeen on the Blue Chip Too who summed it up best. He designated the name "The Point" to be forever changed to a new name more appropriate: "Deuce's Rocking Chair."

It was times like this that really made Jim proud to be a captain in such a magical place. Deuce's ashes were ceremoniously spread over the shallow blue waters encompassing his favorite haunt. Almost magically, six frigate birds, a captain's best friend when looking for dolphin, began circling the memorial service. Flags were flown at half-mast and not a word of usual chatter was heard on the radio during the ride back into port. For some reason the silence said a lot.

The docks at Whale Harbor were old and weathered as well. Just looking at the characteristics of the planking gave the first-timer a feel for the place. Nails were rusted by years of salt air. The sun-bleached planks were stained with drops of fish blood. For so early in the morning, the place was humming with activity.

One after another, the diesels on each charter boat roared to life. They each had their own distinct sound. Low-pitched rumblings intermixed with the gurgling of exhaust waters. It was unproven, but well accepted that certain boats did have a better fish-raising ability by nothing more than a superior harmonic hum.

During the granddaddy of tournaments, the Islamorada

A Bertram sport-fisherman heads out for a day of fishing.

Sailfish Tournament two years earlier, Jim's boat had taken an exceptional five-fish lead the first day. When they returned to the docks that night, Larry had found that one of the propellers had picked up some lobster trap rope. Larry was in the water ready to untangle and cut off the mess when Jim stopped him.

"Is the prop free to turn without damaging the strut," asked Jim.

"Yeah, she's just wrapped neatly around the shaft," said Larry, still treading in the water.

"Let's leave it until Sunday then."

Even with the risk of prop damage, the $30,000 in Calcutta prize money convinced Jim to let it be.

"If the sails like the way it sounds, let's not fool with it," said Jim. When word got out after they took first place, it was the talk of the town for some time.

Snapping out of his walk down memory lane, Jim realized it was time to get to work and get his boat ready for the day's charter.

As they climbed onto the boat, they quickly went into a well-rehearsed routine to prepare themselves for a day of fishing. Larry would prepare the baits and fishing tackle. Jim would open up the cabin, check the engine fluids and fire up the twin Detroit Diesels. Like a pilot, Jim would check all systems. With the navigation and electronic equipment operational, he would go below and crank up the generator and turn on the air conditioner. Here, his guest could get a reprieve from the scorching August sun.

With the diesels now warmed up, Jim checked the water temperature in the port engine. It was still running eight degrees warmer than the starboard. The next down day, he would have to clean out the heat exchanger, as it was probably clogged with seaweed.

Jim had bought his 46-foot Bertram from a widow up in St. Augustine, Florida, eight years before. Her husband's passion had been the ocean. The boat's beauty and function had been meticulously maintained. The widow knew she would miss the boat. It was filled with fond memories, trips to the Bahamas and the long cruise to Cape Hatteras. At least she knew that Jim would be a good steward and treat the old boat like the lady she was.

It was an older boat, built in 1979 when Bertram Yachts was still in its glory days. The one condition she had made on the sale was that the name of the boat remain unchanged. Jim agreed to keep the name Mystic Lady, out of respect for the old couple. They had first met many summers ago, at the mystic Connecticut shore. He had named the boat in her honor.

Last October, Jim took the boat up to Miami, to Merrill-Stevens Dry Dock Company, and had her pulled out of the water. They spent a solid two weeks scraping and sanding. They adorned her with three thick coats of high-gloss white paint.

Jim replaced much of the teakwood with a new high-tech plastic called Star Board. This helped cut down on the demanding maintenance required by teak. Looks were important in his business. Tourists paying $950 for a full-day charter were naturally attracted to a clean, well-maintained boat.

At 7 a.m. a young couple in their early 20s approached the boat. "Hi, my name is Randy and this is my wife, Elaine." As Randy said the word "wife," both Randy and Elaine turned to each other and beamed.

No doubt about it, honeymooners, Jim thought, as he gave Larry a look and a smile.

"Welcome aboard, I'm Jim and this is Larry."

With pleasantries exchanged and everything loaded, Larry untied the dock lines and Jim went up to the fly bridge located over the main cabin.

Islamorada hosted one of the largest charter fleets anywhere in the world. With most trips beginning at the same time, it looked like an armada heading for battle, as the huge fleet left their slips and jockeyed for position in the channel.

Randy and Elaine lived in Cedar Rapids and had never been on a fishing boat so large. Randy was amazed at how effortlessly Jim maneuvered the large vessel in such tight quarters. Jim never touched the wheel, as he slowly walked the engines in and out of gear.

As they cleared the dock, Jim said, "Come on up the ladder to the fly bridge, you'll enjoy the view."

With the expedition under way, Jim was under no obligation to entertain his passengers. Many captains would prefer to be left alone and just find fish. Not Jim, he would launch in to his usual spiel, explaining in detail the beauty and history before them. Larry would sometimes kid him and say he was going to tape it and sell it to the Tourist Development Council.

Small talk continued as they slid across the mirror-like water and entered Hawk's Channel. Randy inhaled deeply and took in the distinct smell of the salt air. As they began to leave land behind them, Elaine could not believe the beauty. With the sun rising on their left, the morning was one of the most peaceful she could remember.

Elaine asked Jim, "It sure is nice here, but to tell you the truth we're a little disappointed. We came down here to relax in the sun, where are all the beaches?"

Jim explained, "The reason we have so few beaches is because of the reefs. They're located about three miles from shore and they break up the wave action. You need the pounding of waves to make a beach."

He pointed at the color fish finder and showed them how the bottom was actually rising as they ventured farther from land and approached the reefs.

"Here is where you will find the true beauty of the Keys," said Jim.

Jim's eyes constantly scanned the horizon. Finally, a smile broke across his face. About half a mile away he thought he saw birds diving. He corrected his course.

"Larry, get the cast-net ready, we're going to have live ones today," said Jim.

Getting closer, they could clearly see pelicans diving and fish scurrying on the surface. Jim abandoned the fly bridge and headed up to the tower, which loomed 30 feet in the air. On the tower Jim had full controls and a separate radio. From his high vantage, he could maneuver the transom of his boat to the black cloud in the water.

Below, Jim watched as several silvery barracudas would charge the school from the depths. Frantic fish would leap out of the water, just narrowly missing the razor-sharp teeth of a 4-foot cuda, only to be eaten by birds dive-bombing from above.

As baits broke the surface of the water, a bird would swoop down and eat it. Below, the school huddled closer and closer in a tight ball for protection. This made things easier for mates armed with a cast net.

"Now, 7 o'clock, 10 feet back!" Jim shouted. Larry tossed his net in a perfect spiral, opening almost to its maximum of 24 feet. Randy could not believe how effortless Larry made it look. With lead weights sewn along the outside ring, the net was quite heavy. The art of throwing a cast net is something passed down from captain to mate.

Larry continued to let out line until he was sure the net made it almost 15 feet below, to the sandy bottom. Then with a large tug, he quickly retrieved the net, tossing it on the deck. The bounty was immense. Cigar minnows covered the deck. Larry quickly opened the live bait well and herded the silvery bouncing fish into the hold.

As Jim returned to the fly bridge he got on his radio. "Challenger, this is Mystic Lady. You copy, Rob?"

After a succinct pause the radio fired back, "Yeah,

Jim, go to 88." Jim switched the radio from Channel 79 to 88.

"Rob, I'm at the patch off E-Marker. We have a nice school of cigars here. I'll keep tossing sand and keep them interested if you want to make it over here," said Jim.

"Be right over. Challenger, standing by on 79." Capt. Rob Dixon was at Davis Reef also in search of bait. He was less than a mile away. It was not long before he backed his transom close to the Mystic Lady and his mate Chris tossed his net, also opening in an impressive spiral.

One thing Jim truly loved about his job was how everyone helped each other. Just when you were having a tough day, a friend would bail you out. With a few exceptions, the captains got along great and worked together as a team. As a group they had synergy and formed one big net spread over the waters in their hunting grounds.

With their live wells full of frisky bait, Jim pointed the bow at 150 degrees and headed southeasterly. In the winter months, the boats never ventured far from the reef line. They went after the abundant snapper and grouper on the reef as well as the sailfish, wahoo and kingfish just off the edge of the reef. In the summer months, they were in search of a different prey, the hunter of the ocean, the dolphin.

This was the beautiful blue, green-colored fish, not the bottle-nosed "Flipper" as everyone first imagines. In Hawaii they called the fish mahi mahi; in local restaurants the name was also catching on. Wait staffs tired of always having to explain that they were not serving porpoise.

Dolphin could have been anywhere. The art of finding them was like a hunter combing the forest for the slightest footprint or sign. Offshore, this forest changes daily. With each new storm and front that passed through, the dolphin would move. Some days they were out 12 miles, some days 30. But each day began the same, looking for signs.

Randy noticed the sun coming up on the port side of the

boat, he thought about it, then asked Jim, "Why are we heading more to the south instead of directly east out to sea?"

Jim answered, "Probably because we host the southernmost point in the continental U.S., most people think the Keys go south. In all actuality, though, the island chain follows one another more westerly, hence the name Key West, for the westernmost key. The Gulf Stream moves northeast at a good clip, usually at least three knots. By heading south, we get to deeper water faster."

Jim began his usual ritual of periodically scanning the horizon with his 70x50 powered binoculars. He never got too excited until he hit the true cobalt blue water of the Gulf Stream. He pointed this out to Randy and Elaine.

With the water so calm he could notice the slightest movement on the water for a great distance. At 2 o'clock he saw some large ripples on the surface. Jim quickly adjusted his autopilot a few degrees to starboard. As they approached, he climbed up the aluminum ladder leading up to his tower.

On calm days, the tower climb was a cakewalk. In 7-foot seas, Jim would have to hold on for dear life as he perilously made the climb. The aluminum bars would become quite slippery from the constant salt spray and the rocking torque of the waves would create a pendulum effect the higher one climbed up the tower.

Looking down from the tower, Jim could see that it was only a lone loggerhead sea turtle in search of jellyfish. Randy took several pictures of the 4-foot turtle. It almost appeared prehistoric compared to the small turtles he had collected in the creek behind his house.

Jim continued to search the waters around the turtle. Many times a nice school of dolphin would stay with a loggerhead. This time, however, the search was futile; they continued on.

With all the lines rigged with their favorite lures, the gleaming gold Penn International reels were set out on their appropriate rod holders. The "Illander Lure" was set out on the left (port) outrigger.

This was Jim's most productive bait. It had a polished chrome weight, shaped like a bullet attached to a colored skirt. The lure was then slipped over a fat horse (large) ballyhoo. The weight would cause the rig to run just below the surface. On this lure, they had caught their heaviest and largest percentage of dolphin, marlin and wahoo.

On the center two flat lines, located on the rear corners of the transom, Larry set out his most beloved schoolie baits, the Dolphin Jr. on the port and the Dolphin Sr. on the starboard. These lures attracted the bread and butter of the charter fleet, the smaller, more numerous schoolie dolphins.

With only the starboard outrigger left, Larry called Elaine down from the fly bridge. He opened a plastic box filled with a myriad of different colored rubber skirts. Skirts were rubber lures that go over rigged baits such as ballyhoo. As became the tradition on the Mystic Lady, the women always picked out this last lure and color.

Elaine picked a dark burgundy-colored skirt, which Larry slid over the ballyhoo. He tossed it over the side and attached it to the starboard outrigger. Fishermen had a saying: bright days, bright lures; dull days, dull lures. The color Elaine had picked went against the rules for this bright and cloudless day. Larry thought to himself that he should have recommended a bright chartreuse color instead.

With the couple now down in the cockpit, Larry began his usual speech. He explained how to properly fight and land large fish. He did a good job going over the basics without ever insulting the most avid outdoorsman. The times when he had experienced guests aboard and had not given Fishing 101, he would always pay for it. At the end of the day the lines would be a mess. It was a lot easier to give the short course, even if he sometimes felt like a flight attendant prior to takeoff.

CHAPTER SIX

I t was while he was training armed guerrillas in Angola that Javier Suarez first learned of knat. In Africa, men would labor for hours in deplorable conditions without complaint. Insects would be covering their dark, sweaty faces in blistering heat yet they would work on, sometimes singing.

At first Suarez had thought it was the effect of superior genetics, brought on by generations born and bred in this equatorial hell. Later he learned that it was what the natives were chewing that got them through their grueling day.

The knat shrub had a slender trunk with smooth thin bark. The lancet-shaped leaves began life a reddish green, then turned a russet yellow green later in life. In some areas of Africa with frost, the shrub grew no higher than 1.5 meters, but in places where rainfall was more plentiful, like the highlands of Ethiopia, knat trees would reach 20 meters.

For generations the tender, fresh knat leaves had been used as a narcotic stimulant. Although some people drank knat in the form of tea or a juice, the most popular method by far was chewing, similar to chewing tobacco.

For many hard laborers in Africa, knat was chewed from sun up to sunset. It had proven itself as a powerful stimulant, capable of making people feel more energetic and alert. It is thought to enhance concentration, reduce hunger and fatigue; it was even used for treating notable diseases.

The difficult part was turning a leaf such as knat, which quickly looses potency, into a powder that could easily be transported. Thankfully, technology imported from Bolivia provided the means to build an efficient processing plant in Ethiopia.

With growing civil unrest in Cuba, the faltering president was desperate to hold on to his failing dictatorship at any cost. With Javier Suarez's plan, known as "Agua Dulce," the president was easily convinced.

Adding knat to Cuba's drinking water had positive effects almost overnight. It had started as a small-scale experiment in Cardenas. Productivity numbers clearly showed impressive gains in factories where knat was introduced.

Workers seemed happier, working long hours without complaint. In six months the scope of the experiment had increased. Except for isolated instances where citizens appeared to walk around in a fog-like trance, all results were positive. Even violent crimes were sharply curtailed.

Although the chief scientist, Ernesto Gonzalez pleaded for more time to study the adverse and addictive effects, it was time to take the plan national.

CHAPTER SEVEN

With the reef well behind him, Jim set the autopilot on a course for the "Hump." The "Hump" as local fishermen called it, was a 300-foot deep-sea mount, elevating from a surrounding depth of 600 feet. As the swift moving body of water in the Gulf Stream hit this mount on the ocean bottom, a large upwelling occurred. Huge schools of tuna, amberjack and sharks would gather there, feeding on the nutrient-rich soup teeming with smaller baitfish. Fishermen were people of habit, and heading for the "Hump" on the way out to deeper water had been Jim's habit for a very long time. Every day he automatically headed first to the "Hump."

They were 11 miles out when both Jim and Larry saw the birds. At the "Hump," you could always count on the bonita birds feeding on the tuna's leftover scraps.

"Elaine, quick, look at all the birds!" Randy said excitedly.

Elaine, who had been relaxing and taking in the sun, quickly rose to her feet. Randy and Elaine climbed the ladder to the fly bridge to get a better look.

"What the heck are they all doing here? There must be hundreds of birds?" Randy said.

"Ah, don't get too excited," replied Jim. " Birds are always a good sign, but these guys are always here and they are not over dolphin, they're just here for the "Hump buffet." Never know what's hanging around the perimeter, though, we'll just cruise around and see what happens," said Jim.

As if on cue, the starboard outrigger made a loud pop and the line quickly pulled tight. The rod immediately began to bend and the reel's bearings started screaming a loud, torturous clicking noise. For a moment it almost sounded like the heavy reel would implode, as line peeled from it with unimaginable quickness.

Larry just smiled and screamed, "FISH ON!" He directed Randy to lift the rod from the holder and sit down in the fighting chair.

Jim backed off the throttles a little, but continued to keep the boat moving forward. As Jim positioned the fish directly behind the boat, Randy began pumping as Larry had instructed. Larry looked like a weightlifting coach, standing next to his pupil. As Randy strained to slow down the fish, Larry told him to "pull up, reel down." The rod tip was pulled high into the air and then Randy would reel quickly as the tip was lowered toward the water.

The minutes seemed like an eternity to Randy. The scorching tropical sun relentlessly took a toll on the angler's body. Every pore in Randy's skin opened up and began pumping out a salty transudation. The gamefish on the other end of line appeared to be winning Round One of this contest. With Larry still coaching, there would be many more rounds in the fight.

Randy's arms began to stiffen first. His arm muscles began to suffer from a distinct lack of oxygen. Lactic acid chemicals began to build in his tissues. Feeling as if he would not last much longer, he started to pump with even more force.

"Don't muscle him!" scolded Larry. "Be gentle, but firm. Give him line when he turns and runs. Wait for him to slow down, then start pumping again."

It always amazed Jim just how excited Larry could get. For such a mild-mannered guy, he turned into a drill sergeant when the fish hit the fan. Some customers did not know how to take it, but for the most part everyone knew he was doing it for their best interest. At the end of the day, when they would have twice as many quality fish as everyone else back at the dock, they knew the sometimes humbling experience had been well worth it.

The angle of the line to the water suddenly grew more slanted. Agitated, the fish broke the water for the first time. About 100 yards behind the boat, the gigantic dolphin flipped in the air, shaking its head wildly in order to free itself. A moment later the fish submerged, leaving behind a hole in the water filled with boiling white foam.

"BOW TO THE FISH, BOW TO THE FISH!" Larry shouted. Randy remembered how Larry had told him to lower the rod tip to the water when the fish jumps into the air. Larry thought it was amazing that a fish that had probably never been at the other end of a hook and line was always so predictable. It was as if they were programmed somehow to elude capture even by man.

As Randy continued his struggle, Larry went to work clearing the deck. He picked up chunks of ballyhoo from the deck. He had Elaine put a small drink cooler in the cabin. With a clean, safe place to work, he lifted the gaff from its holder.

"Coming around the port side, Lare," Jim said. As the fish made one more dash along the port side of the boat, Jim quickly pushed the throttles forward and spun the boat, keeping the fish behind the transom.

"Hot damn, looks like a super slammer," said Larry.

As the fish closed to about 20 feet behind the boat, Larry expertly positioned himself and his gaff. The gaff man could make or break the engagement. With a fish this powerful you usually only had one shot.

Larry could predict how the fish would react by its coloration. If the dolphin was neon blue and lit up, it was still green and had too much fight left in him. It would be best to let the fish tire some more, before gaffing it. If the fish looked more a dull yellow and begun doing the "death spiral," making lazy circles, the fight would soon be over.

Larry would lead the fish to the boat while holding the leader; it was important to be smooth. He would make it a point to never let the fish's head raise out of the water. When the fish came alongside the boat, it was important to position the sharp hook of the gaff just ahead of the fish. When the fish sees the gaff, it will usually begin to lunge forward. If done right, the gaff should hit home in the fish's head, just behind the eye.

At the perfect moment, Larry effortlessly gaffed the fish and heaved him into the open icebox. Immediately all hell broke loose as the fish jumped out of the ice cold water and began slamming violently on the deck. Everyone stood back as Larry slid the angry fish back into the fish box, full of slushy ice and cold salt water.

With the fish safely in the cooler, yet still thrashing to get out, Randy put the rod back in the holder.

"Big fish like this can do a whole lot of damage when they hit the deck. That's why they're called 'slammers,' " said Larry.

"Hot damn! Can you believe that fish … it is huge!" said Randy. Larry and Randy gave each other high-fives and Elaine handed her proud man an ice-cold Miller Lite. For Jim and Larry, this was all in a day's work. For Elaine and Randy, this 48-pound bull dolphin was the largest fish they had ever seen, much less caught.

Without a word, Jim looked down from the fly bridge and met Larry's eyes. They both looked at the bait the dolphin had chosen, then looked at each other and smiled. It had been the wrong color. The fish hit the dark lure Elaine had chosen and it was a bright day. They just nodded their heads as another fisherman's tale got shot full of holes.

The hunt resumed. In no time, Jim spotted another floating board about a half-mile away. As they approached, Jim, perched high in his tower, could not see any fish.

"Board looks great, it's an old 4-by-4. Been in the water a while, too. It is loaded with crustaceans and barnacles. No fish, though. Better go deep, Lare," Jim said.

Larry reached in the live well. Firmly grasping a large cigar minnow, he pinned the fish just behind the anal opening with the live bait hook. Tossing the bait, it frantically hit water and, as they wanted, dove deep.

For several minutes nothing happened. Larry just kept feeding out line. All of a sudden all the slack was gone and the line was tight. "Think I've got something here, Randy get this bad boy to the surface," said Larry.

The line started to peel off the reel. "Feels like a nice one, I better set the hook," Randy said. Flipping the reel's bail closed, Randy reeled in all the slack and then set the hook.

Just as Jim had suspected, a school was down deep. As Randy slowly got the fish up, the school followed. In a matter of minutes all hell was breaking loose. Fish were flopping on the deck.

"Be sure to keep at least one fish in the water at all times. That will hold the school close to the boat," said Larry.

Larry could not get them in the boat fast enough. Lifting and gaffing the fish, he brought them in, while Jim came down and helped by tossing out fresh bait.

"What do you think, Lare, by my count we need two more to limit out," asked Jim.

"I counted 39," replied Larry.

"Randy, you do the honors of bringing in the last fish," said Jim.

Once they hit their limit of 10 fish per person, it was time to head home.

The ride home was uneventful. Randy and Elaine escaped the late afternoon heat and retreated into the cool air-conditioned cabin.

Larry began the process of cleaning everything with soap and fresh water. When the boat was ready for another day of fishing, Larry went back into the cabin to stow the rods. In the comfort of the cabin, he found Randy and Elaine both asleep.

The chatter on the radio had been quiet for some time. With the exception of a few half-day charters, the fleet was all heading home. Alone on the bridge, Jim sipped on a cold iced tea. His shirt was damp from the late afternoon heat. With nothing to listen to except the steady hum of the diesels, Jim's mind went back to the article he read earlier that morning.

So they are finally giving up on our boys, Jim thought, remembering who he, too, had to leave behind enemy lines.

Only Jim's closest friends knew he had been a Navy Seal. It was not something that he spoke of freely, and even his mind refrained from dwelling on it. Sure, he was proud of what he had accomplished, but reflecting on this part of his life came at the expense of much torment.

Unlike the many books written about Navy Seals, in truth it was very improbable that a Seal would have any distinguishing marks, such as a tattoo. With their primary place of operation behind enemy lines, the less evidence the better. However, Jim proudly wore the traditional black onyx ring and a gold Rolex watch. It was a little flashy for Jim's casual style, but to a Seal it was as good as a tattoo.

Momentarily fixing his eyes on the black of his ring, Jim reflected. John Kelly, damn ... how old would you be now? Forty-nine ... You were the best, my friend. Sure was hard to leave you there.

They were only exuberant young boys when they had qualified for BUD (Basic Underwater Demolition) training in Corpus Christi, Texas. Jim could almost smell the muddy rain-soaked camp that had molded them into the men they had become. They developed character and tapped an internal strength they had not previously known. Then they went to war.

The three had gone through training together. John Kelly was a medium-built, tough Irish kid from Boston. He had red hair and a light complexion. Ricardo Balart, quite the opposite, was a wild Cuban-born-but-damn-proud-to-be-American boy. Then there was the kid next door, Jim Riley.

All of them had come close to cracking during Hell Week, but by leaning on each other they had made it through. Jim would never forget the night the three received the much-revered pinning of the badge. It sure hurt like hell, but it was a medal that could never be forgotten or taken away.

Surviving treacherous duty in Vietnam, in 1972, the three were reunited on Andros Island, Bahamas. They were part of the famous Team One. Jim's team became a living science project and had been training on arming and disarming tactical nuclear weapons on sunken nuke subs.

They were almost beginning to forget life behind enemy lines when they received orders to hop on a Huey to join the carrier attack class 59, US Forrestal. There they were debriefed on a new crisis brewing close to home in Havana Harbor.

United States satellites had detected what appeared to be yet another missile crisis afoot in Cuba. More than sixty Russian vessels were already in Havana Harbor and what looked to be missiles were being unloaded. Not wanting to once again panic the American public, they needed to go in for a closer, clandestine look.

Loaded for bear, the three were transferred to the nuclear submarine USS Sand Lance (SSN-660). It was Cmdr. William A Kennington's first challenging mission since the submarine was commissioned on September 25, 1971. The sub silently slipped into Havana Harbor and quickly began acquiring transmissions validating Washington's worst fears.

Unexpectedly, alarms began flashing in the submarine's control panels; the reactor was overheating. Unable to disengage the reactor, Commander Kennington sat her down on the bottom, where her reactor continued to heat up.

To Jim it felt like yesterday, he could feel the sudden coolness of the water as the three had to exit through the escape hatch and find the problem. It was a hazard of operation in shallow water. The main cooling intake tube was completely blocked with silt. It took several hours, but the tube was cleaned and once again the flow of cool water was restored to the reactor.

Even in dive gear, Jim could hear and feel a sudden ping pierce his body. The sound came from the direction of their only escape from Havana Harbor. Looking in the direction of the sharp cacophony, Jim stretched the limits of his visibility. Confirming his apprehension, the sound originated from a sierra-class Russian attack sub. The enemy submarine had taken up residence not more than 100 yards behind the USS Sand Lance.

Once detected, the commander's order was to get the sub out of the harbor at all cost. The Russians, however, wanted nothing less than complete surrender. Invading the sovereign Cuban waters was an act of war!

As the standoff continued, several tense hours passed. Jim remembered his conversation. With fire in his belly, Jim said, "We can do it, Commander. We have the explosives and we can disable that sierra."

"That's all we need," answered Commander Kennington. "Blow up a Russian sub in Cuba with all these nukes around and we will have World War III."

"They won't want to die, Commander. We'll just scare 'em a little, that's all."

With much trepidation, the commander agreed to consider Riley's plan. Navy Seals were taught to improvise. When sent on a mission they were programmed to interpret the situation and react. Without rigid guidelines or thick policy manuals, they had proven themselves highly effective in combat situations.

It took Jim less than 10 minutes to draw out his plan. They would slip into the water and attach magnetic explosives to the sub's steering controls. The coolant and the ballast intake ports would be sealed. They would clip the communications antenna and weld shut the emergency hatch.

Using ship-to-ship communications they would contact the Ruskies and give them no choice but to stay put, allowing the hobbled U.S. submarine to leave the port.

The plan was simple and involved only the three divers. Commander Kennington agreed it was their best likelihood of escape. Surrendering one of the Navy's latest nuclear submarines was out of the question. If all else failed, they would have no choice but to evacuate as best they could and scuttle her.

Taking a deep breath and nodding, Jim decided that he needed to take his mind off the past. You brave idiot, so quick to offer your men. If only we'd been more damn careful. Sorry, John old boy, gritting his teeth he turned for the head pin at Whale Harbor. He popped in a Jimmy Buffett cassette and entered the narrow channel for home as the song "A Pirate Looks at Forty," played over the bridge speakers. The sound was garbled from the hundreds of times of use, but it served Jim well and relaxed him.

CHAPTER EIGHT

In the town of Santa Lucia, on the northern shore of Cuba, a rooster crowed as a dark sky began to reveal a hint of red and purple far to the East. Ricardo Balart had already been up for several hours. His wife, Ana, turned over in bed and asked, "How's it coming, Ricardo?"

"Not bad, Ana, just a few more pieces to this crazy puzzle."

As Ana rose from bed to make some coffee, she could not believe the stacks of documents spread all over her tiny bedroom floor. Her whole family could be shot and would at the very least be thrown in jail forever if the authorities ever got wind of this.

As the smell of the strong Cuban coffee began to permeate throughout the house, Ana put down a small cup in front of Ricardo. He drank the coffee like a shot of whiskey, not even taking his eyes off the papers before him..

"I'm almost finished," he said. "I've been working for three months and finally I have most of the details. But what if I've made a mistake? If I've left out some small but important detail, my brother could be a dead man."

"If that happens, you know you will have done your best. That's what counts," Ana said as she rubbed his shoulders.

Ricardo had been working feverishly transcribing pages of notes into a code. It was a simple code, as codes go. Using a Spanish version of the Hemingway's, "Old Man and the Sea," Ricardo would find the word or letter he wanted to use in the book. He would then convert the word to a code such as P118W17, which meant page 118, the 17th word. For some hard-to-find words the code could be broken into letters, P14W3L3, for page 14 of the book, the third word and the third letter of that word.

The end result was a code, which was unbreakable unless you had the same printing of the same book. Having gotten the idea from a novel, his brother in the United States had sent the book to him six years earlier. It was one of the few American books allowed in Cuba, thanks to the reverence the Cuban people had for Papa Hemingway. Once established, the code gave the brothers freedom to communicate between the two countries that few people could experience.

Through his family and with his job, Ricardo had access to the inner workings of Basanta's regime, but the details seemed endless. He was officially a member of "The Cuban Communist Party," but with the exception of a few people he was always treated as an outsider.

His Aunt, Mirta Diaz Balart had divorced Basanta in 1959, when Ricardo was just 7 years old. It was hard to recall the faint memories of the great Adolfo that he had known.

Adolfo Basanta was the current ruling dictator of Cuba. With the exception of a small minority, the "great" leader was equally despised by all of his countrymen. Whatever happened to the ideals Adolfo had in his early years? As a child, he remembered how proud he had been to tell people that Adolfo was his uncle. What devil had entered the dictator's soul and corrupted such a pure spirit?

Ricardo disrobed and stepped into the shower. As usual, the water was cold. With the dwindling supply of petroleum, hot water heaters were not a welcome appliance. It was hard to believe that Basanta actually enlisted a committee promoting the taking of cold showers to be for the greater good, "The Cause."

What bullshit! thought Ricardo as he quickly bathed.

He put on his uniform and looked in the mirror as he finished getting ready. He wondered how much longer it would be business as usual in Cuba. With the rafters in 1994, he thought that the people had endured enough. But riots were quickly quieted. Basanta promised to allow vendors freedom from black-market punishment, and life went back to normal. How much longer would normal be considered acceptable?

Staring at his aging face in the mirror, Ricardo began thinking to himself: In America they could only dream of education like ours, 95 percent literate! The best health care in the world and we have to take cold showers and eat meat only once every other week. What the hell for!

Slamming his clinched fist on the bathroom counter he said, "For Basanta, for his ego, that was why. You're too damn proud to give in and admit that we were wrong, that communism does not work!"

Ricardo got on his rusty, worn-out Russian-made bike and rode the 2 miles to the docks. As captain of the 126-foot Cuban coast guard ship, "El Matador," Ricardo was well respected by his men. As he boarded his ship his shirt was already damp with perspiration from the early-morning humidity. Once on deck, the crew quickly saluted and stepped aside. His yeoman immediately set coffee down at his side and began organizing Ricardo's morning reports for him.

Ricardo gave orders and his crew quickly obeyed. They were out of the harbor in short order. The radio suddenly came to life. A fishing boat had spotted what they thought was a raft. Pedro, the navigation officer, plotted the course and determined it would take them 40 minutes to reach 20 miles out on the flat, calm sea.

Ricardo loved the ocean. It was the one thing in life that had not let him down. As unpredictable and unforgiving as it had been, it had never made any promises it did not keep. He immediately felt sorry for the poor bastards who tried to make it to Florida during this time of year with sometimes flat and dead calm seas.

With the right current and light winds you could make the trip to Florida in four or five days. In these doldrums days, you could spend three days and not lose sight of land. How desperate they must be to try anyway!

"Balsero, 2 o'clock," shouted the watch commander.

"Starboard, 10 degrees," ordered Captain Balart. Approaching, he found what he had already seen too often. The raft, hastily made up of truck tire tubes with rope and plywood, was seaworthy enough, but there were no signs of food, water or life. He could search but he was sure what he would find.

When the body dehydrates the tongue begins to swell, the eyes enter far into the sockets, the tongue turns black in the final stages. For most, the mind thankfully shuts down first. As Ricardo entered his report in his log, he thought back to the many "Balseros" he had found with black, swollen tongues. Wish I could put old Adolfo on a piece of wood until his tongue turned black, he thought.

For Ricardo, the day could not pass quickly enough. All he could think of was the important fax he was waiting to send. As the time for transmission approached, he relieved his helmsman and watchman to the dining quarters and took control of the helm. As he had done on numerous occasions, he quietly slipped the vessel out of his normal patrol area.

At precisely 18:00 he pushed the send button on his Nav-Fax. This transmission would be picked up by anyone who happened to be monitoring the channel. The Nav-Fax at the Navy Intelligence Communications Center in Florida City picked up the satellite send signal and went into the receive mode.

In the heart of Havana, Major Javier Suarez was notified of yet another transmission of gibberish. For months now they had been trying to crack the code. They had triangulated the transmission to within 3 square miles. Believing it was being sent from someone right on the beach, a patrol was once again dispatched to a deserted beach.

Once the transmission was complete, Ricardo quickly returned to his assigned patrol area. This should be the last for a while. Now he had to wait for the reply. He struck a match, lit the papers he had just sent, then lit a large robusto cigar. Smiling, he sat back, a huge weight lifted from his shoulders.

Within 20 minutes the fax had been copied, documented and faxed on a secured line to the Navy base in San Diego. Lt. Commander Charles Balart was waiting by the fax machine. As the last page fell, he quickly began transcribing the code using the Hemingway novel. By 23:10 he had finished.

It was eight years previous when the two brothers had finally spoken. Charlie felt like someone who had been adopted and never knew his siblings. He had left Cuba at only 10 years old when things had started to get heated. His mother sent him to Miami with the Catholic Church, Operation Pedro Pan. She decided to stay behind with her youngest son, Ricardo Balart.

It had been difficult growing up with strangers in Miami. At the request of his mother, a family who they had barely known took him in. They were good to him, and treated him like one of their own. His Christian name was Carlos Manuel Balart, but early on he embraced the American culture and favored being called Charlie. His biological family and his homeland soon faded into distant memories.

When Basanta finally allowed phone calls between the United States and Cuba, it was like a dream to talk to his brother. Their lives were light years apart. Charlie voluntarily went into the Navy after high school. He became a Navy Seal and after finishing college became involved in naval intelligence.

It was amazing that being brought up separately, they were still drawn to careers having to do with the sea. Once they established the code and could communicate, Charlie thought it was uncanny how much alike they both were. Charlie was glad to see that even with all the communist doctrine Ricardo had grown up with, he had seen the truth. Like a mathematical equation with a fatal flaw, the numbers could never add up. Communism did not work.

Charlie's 5-foot-11 frame looked as if it were carefully chiseled from stone. The many hours he had spent in the weight room were evident in his broad shoulders and tapered waist. With his buzz cut hair and clean-shaven face, he definitely looked the part of the Navy officer. He was of light complexion, yet had the look of a fierce Spanish warrior with his dark hair and piercing brown eyes.

After reading the decoded document, Charlie made some notes, then picked up the phone.

"Admiral Franklin, sorry to wake you, sir, but I received the fax we expected. We need to talk."

"I'll meet you at my office in 20 minutes," Franklin replied. The admiral did not bother calling for a car. He slipped on some blue jeans, a shirt and jumped in his own car. Charlie arrived at the office first and made some coffee. Their meeting with the Joint Chiefs of Staff was scheduled for 2 p.m. the next day. Charlie knew it was going to be a long night.

CHAPTER NINE

With a sudden thud, the wheels of the jet hit the tarmac. With the engines being reversed and brakes being applied, the bouncing plane quickly slowed down. Admiral Franklin's eyes opened abruptly from a deep nap as the plane was now taxiing to a waiting car at National Airport in Washington, D.C.

The flight was long and tiring. Both Adm. George Franklin and Lt. Commander Charlie Balart tried sleeping for the first 30 minutes. Charlie then retrieved his laptop and, with the help of Microsoft Office, started making a slick presentation.

A driver was waiting and whisked them to the Pentagon and through the guard gate. Upon entering the building, Charlie could not believe how he felt. His heart was racing. He could feel the perspiration build as he walked down the final hall leading to the meeting room. Turning into the meeting room, he could feel several drops of sweat run from his armpit and down the side of his torso. It felt almost as cold as his hands.

Now in the room, he was shocked to find just an ordinary-looking conference room. He had expected something more grandiose. The people already seated were intimidating enough, though. He had heard of them all, but he had never met them.

After a brief introduction, Admiral Franklin turned the floor over to Charlie. Rising from his chair, Charlie made his way to the small podium in front of the room. Charlie had spoken to larger adudiences before, but as he glanced around the room, he realized that this was by far the most powerful group he had faced. When Charlie began to speak, he started talking way too fast. The words he was thinking just were not flowing smoothly from his lips. After giving a brief run down on his personal background, he looked around and realized he must slow down. With a pause, he took a deep breath and swallowed a gulp of water. Then calmly, he began once more.

"Gentlemen, one of America's greatest fears has come to fruition," Charlie said. "Basanta's nuclear research team has developed and tested a system, that when fully operational, will allow them to produce Intercontinental Ballistic Nuclear Missiles. The project, called Nautilus was named after the first U.S. nuclear powered submarine built in 1954."

Charlie turned and plugged the projection monitor into the communications port on his lap top. On the wall behind him the presentation was displayed.

"On this planet, uranium is not as rare as people might believe. In fact it is more plentiful than both mercury and silver. However, pure enriched uranium, needed to make plutonium, is very difficult to get. In fact, millions of tons would have to be mined in order to get your hands on enough enriched uranium or U-235 to make a single weapon. In each atom of uranium only 0.7 percent is U-235; the rest, 99.3 percent, is U-238, and U-238 is not weapon grade."

"In 1945 the atom bomb in Hiroshima produced 12 kilotons of TNT and killed approximately 100,000 people. With plutonium, processed from enriched uranium, you are capable of making an explosion equal to 1 megaton. This is roughly 10 times more powerful than Hiroshima," explained Charlie.

"Lieutenant, I believe most of us understand the principles of bomb making," interrupted Ken Smith, chief of staff. Clearing his throat and leaning forward, he said, "What we want to know is, how is the son of bitch doing it?" Smith looked at his watch, then back at Charlie.

"Sir, the Cubans have a nuclear physicist working for them named Ernesto Gonzalez," Charlie explained. "Dr. Gonzalez stumbled across a theory and no one knows exactly how he does it, but he has produced pure plutonium. From what our source has been able to find out, he gets the uranium from Japan. Fifty percent of Japan's energy comes from nuclear power plants. The real problem for Japan has been disposing of its waste. With no salt mines to store them in, they went to the free market to find a trade partner. With Cuba in such bad financial shape, Japan almost felt good about supplying Cuba with millions of tons of high-tech products in exchange for them storing nuclear waste. What Doctor Gonzalez developed was a intricate way to extract the enriched uranium, U-235, from the waste uranium."

Charlie pulled up a map of Cuba on his computer. He then pointed at the image the projection monitor displayed on the wall. "This is Havana," he moved the pointer to the North of Cuba and eased the pointer to the East. "This is Santa Lucia, where my brother lives." He moved the cursor further east to a small bay in north central Cuba. "This is Cardenas. This is where Nautilus Project is headquartered. The Cubans put the main building right in the center of town. Within 200 feet, you have a school and a church. Not even the smartest laser bomb we have would risk the publicity. No, gentlemen, here we need a covert operation, led by someone with expert knowledge of the culture and the terrain. I was born 30 miles from this place. I will work with my brother and an ex-Navy Seal named James Riley."

"As you know, my brother is the captain of a Cuban gun boat. Together we plan to meet in the Bahamas, the Cay Sal Bank. Once united, we will transfer the equipment we need to his boat and enter the country under stealth. Together we can silence the fine Doctor Gonzalez and destroy the Nautilus Project laboratory and all its contents. Our plans will make it appear like an experiment gone awry," Charlie said, gaining stature and straightening his posture.

At that point, Ken Smith's aide, Michael O'Donald, spoke up.

"It is strictly against policy for family to work together in such a volatile operation. The entire mission could be ruined over one second wasted to save your brother. I, myself, would want to see a team go in with no emotion, with only the mission before them."

Charlie passionately interrupted. "Then the mission is lost!" Becoming almost cocky he said, "Only my brother can guide us to the exact location. Sure, we could use our intelligence on the island, but one whiff of us knowing about the project and it will be moved overnight. We've seen this before. Every spook we've got working out of our Havana bureau has at least three people assigned full time to them. My brother will do this with no one but me!"

Admiral Franklin put his hand on Charlie's sleeve and said, "Gentlemen, Charlie is not giving you an ultimatum, as he would imply. He has spent many months preparing himself for this assignment. I personally feel there is no other person in the armed forces today better qualified than Lt. Commander Charlie Balart for this task."

Slowly and with reverence, Ken Smith said, "As you may know there are two ways to climb an oak tree. In one way you take a hold of the first branch and start climbing. The other way you take an acorn and sit on it. Gentlemen, we cannot afford to sit on an acorn and wait for an oak tree to grow up our ass. We must stop this thing before it gets any further along. After looking at your résumé it sounds like you're the best damn man for the project. I heard about that job you did for us in Panama; I'm glad to finally meet you, Lt. Commander Balart. Please excuse us for a few minutes and we will let you know. Michael, would you kindly take these gentlemen down to the coffee room."

Charlie felt drained. He had never tried selling a plan he felt so passionately about. In most cases he was only the pawn. He would perform the sortie and many times not even know who was directing him. This mission, he had to admit, was personal.

"That was a hell of a job, son. I think you did it," Admiral Franklin said as they sat down for coffee. Charlie began to relax a bit, as he began to at least breathe again.

A few minutes later, Michael O'Donald came back into the coffee room. Inside Charlie knew he had won his chance. As he entered the room, Ken Smith was smiling and said, "You've got your shot, Lt. Commander Balart. We, of course, can pull the plug, though, if word gets out. I don't need to tell you how sensitive this assignment will be."

"There will be no mission name. There will be no record of this conversation. If the Cubans find you, you'll be just another crazy Cuban, a member of Alpha 66, going back home to make terror. Admiral Franklin will be in charge of every aspect of the mission. Good luck, gentlemen!"

The first few hours of the flight back home were very relaxing. After several hours of much-needed deep sleep Charlie awoke. In a cold sweat, he had a terrible feeling that he would not survive this engagement.

The feeling was nothing new. He never talked about it, but he always had the same sinking feeling before every job. With more and more covert missions under his belt, he was growing more fearful instead of more confident. He felt the odds were no longer in his favor. How many times can you be dealt a hand and always win and not fold?

Charlie was a cautious warrior. In every great hero there is always great fear and apprehension. Staring out the window Charlie remembered reading fear heightens the senses and allows the great ones to survive.

The next morning, Charlie woke up and put on his workout clothes. He ran down the main base road and made his way onto the Pacific Coast Highway. With the sun rising over the mountains, the sky was on fire with a brilliant color of red. He ran down to the beach. The moment Charlie's eyes met the water, he heard the crashing surf and inhaled the briny salt air. In seconds he would become relaxed. The ocean had its cadence, and Charlie could never live far from it.

Every morning Charlie would run 6 miles before breakfast. This morning he ran 8 to burn the extra stress he felt with the burden he had accepted. At 200 yards from the base's side entrance, Charlie, as usual, began to sprint to end his run. This ensured that any remaining tension in his body would surely be burned off like the final blast from a rocket booster before disengagement. His breathing was now labored. His lungs screamed for more oxygen. Passing a bus bench and a yellow fire hydrant, he pretended to cross an imaginary finish line. Now it was time to relax, he began to walk and enjoy his cool-down, still laboring to breathe.

Sitting on the bench was an older gentleman with a gray beard that was neatly groomed. He wore a navy blue jogging suit, but by his hunched demeanor, it was apparent that he was far too frail to be a runner. In his left hand, he held a newspaper, in his right a Styrofoam cup with coffee. For the most part he looked like an ornery condo commando waiting at bay for someone to forget to pick up their dog's excrement or park in the wrong place. He looked peculiar even for Southern California, wearing large sunglasses with white frames and mirrored lenses.

After several minutes Charlie regained his breath.

Doubling back, he began walking for the gate. As he approached the bench, the old man removed his glasses, looked up and with a Jewish accent said, "Young man, do you have the time?"

Turning to his left, Charlie looked up to make eye contact and said, "Sorry, sir, I am not ... Vladimir, what the hell are you doing here?"

Vladimir Polinski, was a retired KGB agent. Charlie had gotten to know him over the past few years exchanging friendly information. As the cold war ended, so did Vladimir's usefulness to his agency. Life in the United States agreed with him. The thought of returning to a dreary life in Russia was not something that he looked forward to. Retiring in San Diego, he had a thriving import-export business shipping computer products back home. After many years of working together, the two adversaries had grown almost fond of each other.

Placing his pointer finger to his lips, to indicate discretion, Vladimir said, "Sit down, Charlie, I have a gift for you."

"But Vladimir, I am not prepared, I have nothing to offer in return."

"Nothing is expected, my friend, this is something special. As you Americans call, a freebie. I was exchanging stories with an old comrade from my sector, when we got to talking about Cuba. I immediately thought of you. He told me about a prisoner that Basanta still has incarcerated in the Mantanzas Political Prison. He has been there for more than 20 years. Our Navy picked him up during a naval exercise in '72. His name is ..."

Vladimir pointed to a corner of his paper where he had written the prisoner's name in large print. "Adolfo is a mad man and I thought your side deserved a break."

Charlie's emotions ran wild. "Thank you, my friend, I will always remember your kindness."

Solemnly, the two men got up and parted company.

CHAPTER TEN

When Charlie arrived in his office, he finished his list of essential equipment and supplies he would need. He then sent the list directly to Admiral Franklin. The admiral would see to it that he had everything he needed within 24 hours.

Grabbing his worn copy of "Old Man and the Sea," he coded another message to his brother. Along with letting him know the mission status, he asked for as much information on the Mantanzas Prison as possible.

He faxed the message to the transmission site, then looked up the number of an old friend down in the Keys. Charlie looked at his watch; it was 10 in the morning Pacific Time. That made it 1 o'clock Eastern time. He figured his buddy would be out fishing, so he dialed his cellular number.

As the line rang, Charlie could tell immediately that it was a bad connection. "Jim," shouted Charlie, "this is Charlie, can you hear me?"

"What, is that you, Charlie? I can barely hear you," answered Jim.

"Yeah, it's me, I need to book your boat, I'm coming to Florida."

"Sure, Charlie, but I can barely hear you. I'm out 18 miles, and almost out of cell range. Can I call you tonight?"

"Sure," answered Charlie.

Today, Jim and Larry had clients on board from Wisconsin. At the very moment Jim was on the phone an outrigger clip popped and the line started peeling off the reel. All of a sudden the second outrigger clip snapped and the other line began screaming. Larry yelled, "FISH ON!" Just like firemen in an old movie, the boat came to life. One of the passengers hopped up and grabbed the rod and set the hook. The other went inside to get the video camera.

"Put that camera down, we got us a double hookup," barked Larry. The passenger quickly sat down the camera and grabbed the rod closest to him. It was bent and screaming. Sitting in his office in California, Charlie was envious, He could hear Jim bellowing out orders to his crew, and he wished he could really go down there just for fun.

Jim tried not yelling into the phone, "Large school, maybe 300 fish, throw 'em some live ones, Lare."

Larry opened the live well and with a small net scooped up about a dozen pilchards and tossed them behind the boat. The water erupted in a frenzy of action. The misplaced pilchards appeared to walk on the water, after one look at the hungry school of Dolphin below them.

Charlie said, "Jim, you got your hands full; we'll talk tonight. Tight lines and good fishing!"

"Thanks, Charlie, talk at you later," said Jim as he pushed the END button on his phone.

Larry wasted no time in gaffing the first fish. Once in the boat, he already had another line ready and tossed it over the transom. In the blink of an eye a large blue green flash rushed in and engulfed the bait.

"Leave the bail open, wait, wait, wait. NOW reel like hell, take out all that slack, set that hook," barked Larry. With another fish on, it was time to boat the next fish.

Jim had it easy. He just stood watch and pointed out fish. The group below quickly became a team as they worked the school. The three actually developed a rhythm. Larry would just point and each player would do what was needed. They caught 20 nice fish, and there were plenty more to be had.

About a half a mile away, Jim could see the Fish Tales coming his way. "Fish Tales, Fish Tales, this the Mystic Lady, do you copy? Over."

"Jimbo, switch and answer on 82," answered Ron.

Jim changed the channel to 82. "Hey, Ron we got a bunch of lifters, I'll hold 'em if you can get over here," said Jim. "Thanks, bud, we have some cranky Germans and an empty cooler. I'll be right over."

A lifter was a term used to describe a schooly dolphin, which was small enough to lift into the boat without the use of a gaff. They made up the bulk of what charter boats had in their coolers at the end of a day. When a dolphin reached 15 or more pounds, they were called gaffers. A gaff would be needed to get them over the side of the boat and into the fish box without the line breaking.

You would have thought the boat was on fire as you looked at the Fish Tales. Black plumes of exhaust smoke came from nowhere as she pulled in her lines and ran full throttle towards the Mystic Lady.

As they approached, Larry could hear Jim talking on the radio high above them, pointing out fish to the other boat. As they got their first hookup, Jim said, "We got all the nice ones, boys, let's head south."

The next two hours were slow. The one drawback of these flat, calm August days was the lack of breeze. On days like this, Jim would keep a dozen towels in the drink cooler. Every few hours, he would pass the ice-cold towels around, and they would wear them like turbans on their heads.

Twenty-five miles out, Jim spotted a small object on the

horizon. He changed course 10 degrees to starboard and made way for it. As he got closer he saw a frigate bird otherwise known as a man-of-war circling high overhead. To an offshore fisherman this was like a rainbow leading to a pot of gold. When this bird's circles begin to tighten, it nearly always meant fish.

When Jim was still several hundred yards away, he called out to Larry, "Better check the baits, Lare, we've got us a raft coming up." Rafts were very common in the Florida Straits; in the last rafter exodus in '94, Jim remembered finding 18 of them in a single day. That summer they had the largest catch of dolphin in recorded history.

In the Gulf Stream, anything that floats becomes an oasis. Tiny crustaceans and barnacles quickly take up residence. Soon small baitfish seek the food and protection of the object. Within about five days, you get triggerfish and tripletail. Soon you have the dolphin, wahoo and even marlin. The once-protective piece of flotsam soon becomes a magnet for any predatory fish looking for any easy meal.

For this reason, a raft is very cherished by almost anyone seeking fish. It is the only good by-product that had come from Basanta, but at such a high cost. Jim had seen them all. Some rafts were nothing more than a few blocks of Styrofoam, others elaborate drums welded in place with sails, a rudder and perhaps even a sea anchor. This saddened Jim. He had found perhaps 100 rafts. On them he had found only a couple dozen survivors. He was far enough North that in most cases thankfully a passing freighter, or a plane from Brothers to the Rescue, a group of Cuban exiles in Miami with volunteer planes, had already found the rafters and rescued them.

As he got closer to this one, he looked but could find no one on board. The makeshift sail, a beige blanket, was torn and in tatters. An empty five-gallon plastic yellow jug lay sideways on top of the raft, rolling back and forth with

During a spectacular Florida Keys sunrise, a mate aboard a charter boat drops anchor prior to casting for bait, readying for a day's fishing.

each swell. Jim looked closely for the markings that would at least ease his mind. At last he found them as he looked with his binoculars. "USCG" was spray-painted in the starboard side in orange day-glow paint. Now he could relax and enjoy catching what had to be lurking below. It always bothered him when he found a raft with no one on board and no Coast Guard markings.

He looked up and noticed the bird had moved slightly to the right. He adjusted his heading to intercept the fish, lining up his baits to swim between the sun the bird and the water. "Larry, keep watch on the port outrigger, we should get a hit just about ...," and before Jim could finish the sentence the line popped out of the outrigger.

This time the line did not just run from the reel. This time the rod bent and for a minute looked as though it would break. The two passengers looked at one another in astonishment and the largest man, about 220 pounds, took hold of the rod. "Set the hook NOW!" barked Larry. The passenger pulled back on the rod and eased down into the fighting chair.

For what seemed like an eternity, the line kept slowly peeling off the reel. The fish was sounding and going deep. It was eerie when the reel finally stopped stripping line.

As soon as it stopped, Larry said, "Start pumping, son!"

The melee had just begun. After 10 minutes of slowly pumping and reeling to regain 100 yards of lost line the fish would take off and again peel off 120 yards more.

The OH-MI, was not far from the Mystic Lady. Even with a boat a mile away, when it stopped, a good captain would take notice. Capt. Bill Kelly got on his radio, "Mystic Lady, this is the OH-MI, you hooked up, Jimbo?"

Jim answered, "Big blue marlin, Bill, she hasn't come up yet, but that's what we got. I'm sure there's some dolphin here, we got us a raft. Come on over and help yourself."

As Bill made his way over, Jim eased the throttles forward to slowly and gently bring the fish up. With a steady pressure the fish began its assent back toward the surface. As the tourist strained, he began to regain more and more line. Having never caught something like this, the tourist had no idea what a physical toll it took on the body. The heavy-set fisherman, with eyes bulging out of their sockets, looked like a heart attack ready to happen. For many minutes, he thought there was no way he would be able to outlast this monster. As more line appeared on the reel, he began to gradually regain his confidence.

The line suddenly went slack. With the tension gone, the fisherman automatically raised the rod tip high into the air. With rocket force, the big blue lunged into the air. "Bow to the fish!" bellowed Jim. The fish began to tail-walk. The regal blue fish violently began shaking its head, trying to free itself, while leaping from the water at the same time. It actually appeared to be walking across the water on his tail. With the video camera rolling, the performance continued.

Twice the fish came close enough to the boat for Larry to touch the 10-foot leader. Each time, however, the fish was still green and would go shooting from the boat with incredible speed. After 1 hour and 20 minutes the fish conceded his fight. The big blue remained motionless as Larry began wiring the fish; he wrapped the leader around his hand. When the fish came along the boat, Jim kept the boat moving at idle speed. Larry grabbed the magnificent animal by its beak and began removing the Islander Lure. With the bait removed, it was time to revive the fish and take some pictures.

Jim came down and brought down the International Billfish Foundation fish tag kit. Jim tagged the fish just behind the dorsal fin on the right side. Not wasting time, he quickly measured the fish's length and girth. Later, taking out a pocket calculator he kept in the tag kit, he squared the girth, then multiplied it by the length in inches. He then divided that by 800 to give him the estimated weight at 429 pounds. He filled out the tag card and with pictures complete, the fish was released unharmed.

Not much else in life gave Jim the feeling he got when he released such a magnificent animal. A little worn from the battle, the tired but healthy fish silently slipped back into the deep blue water. The last thing Jim saw was the huge black eye staring at him, as the animal faded away. Jim's reverence for billfish ran deep. To him a billfish was not a fish at all but an animal with spirit and personality. He felt like an equal, both hunters of the blue water, as he would stare eye to eye with one. It was a bond few people got to experience.

Not many years ago, people would keep billfish for trophies. Today they were almost always released. With proper measurements, a replica mount is made from fiberglass and the fish got to swim off and fight another day. If some impecunious guy did show up at the docks with a billfish, it had better died in the battle or have been a world record or a mob lynching might take place. World-record contenders were still kept in order to be authenticated. The billfish, unless smoked, is absolutely no good for table fare.

With pictures and fantastic memories, Jim switched the auto pilot on and started back to port. The ride home would be long, and it gave Jim time to think. He wondered about his old friend Charlie Balart. Charlie was one of Jim's closest friends. Through all the horrors of war, the two had somehow survived.

Their personalities were totally different. Charlie was flamboyant and Jim was just the opposite, low-key. Jimmy Buffett had many songs that were all favorites to Jim. If he had to pick just one song to be his favorite, it would be impossible.

It all depended on his current state of mind.

One verse, though, that came closest to describing Jim Riley was an old favorite. The verse from the song "The Wino and I Know" went, "I'm just trying to get by, being quiet and shy, in a world full of push n' shove."

Most people would never think of Jim as shy, but if he had his way, he would much rather be out here, fishing and living life as Buffett said in "Three quarter Thyme."

Charlie, on the other hand, was a wild man. Charlie would do anything just to make a statement. Before he moved to the West Coast, he would throw a "Christmas in July" party in Miami every year. For 12 straight years it became a cherished reunion for all the old friends from the Navy. He would rent tuxedoes, put up Christmas trees. He would even put up lights and have a huge lighted Santa on his lawn. Jim would not miss the party for the world.

Charlie was married once, but his ex-wife Lisa could not handle the pressure. Once Charlie got wrapped up in the intelligence business, he turned his boundless kinetic energy toward his work. He would disappear for weeks at a time. It was not a job conducive to a good marriage. It was sad to see them break up. Lisa was a good person and Jim had hoped that somehow they could work things out.

He had tried to explain to Lisa that the crazy side of Charlie was only a facade. It was Charlie's way of hiding his pain. He had only memories of a family that had meant the world to him. Separated by 90 miles of ocean, Cuba might as well have been on the other side of the planet. Jim was one of the few friends Charlie had who really understood that.

As Jim returned to the Whale Harbor Marina and finished cleaning the boat, he could not wait to get home and call his old friend.

CHAPTER ELEVEN

As the phone rang, Linda took her spoon out of the spaghetti sauce and picked up the phone. Linda had just heard the truck pull up and the dog started to bark. "Hi, Charlie, good timing, Jim just pulled up."

"Great, he said he was going to call me tonight, but I was just leaving the office and thought I would try him instead," said Charlie.

"No problem, he'll be right up," said Linda.

"Thanks, Linda, can' t wait to see you guys again. Sure miss those great weekends with you both in the Keys."

"Yeah, we do too. Jim called, he said you might be coming. ... Take care, here's Jim," said Linda, handing off the phone.

"Charles, how the hell you been?"

"Not bad, but the Cuban food here sucks and the ground shakes and rattles. Feels like we're gonna fall right into the ocean out here. It gets me a little nervous, miss that terra firma of good old Florida coral rock. How's your week look? I need to book you for at least four days."

Jim got out his scheduling book. As he opened it up he noticed he was booked solid for the next three weeks.

"Four days, Charlie, are you nuts, what the hell you want to fish for four days for?"

"I'll explain when I get down. It's business, pleasure and much more, Jim," said Charlie. Jim could hear the seriousness in his voice and understood.

"Well, I'm wide open. You tell me when, and I'll work around it," said Jim.

"My plane lands tomorrow afternoon at 4. I can go over all the details when I get there. Jim, remember Havana Harbor, 1972; I'm really going to need your help," said Charlie.

Jim paused, thinking just how difficult it would be to reschedule all of those bookings to other charter boats, then said, "See ya' tomorrow. Want me to pick you up at the airport?"

"Thanks, Jim, but I'll be flying into Homestead. I'll get a G-Ride," said Charlie.

Jim smiled; a government car never did suit Charlie. A Jeep with no top would be much more his style.

After dinner Linda got out fresh linen and thought how nice it would be to watch Jim and Charlie laugh again, just like the old days. Maybe it would help Jim and Linda to feel closer, reminiscing about the past. It amazed Linda how grown men could somehow transcend time and revert to an age-old past. They would tell the same old jokes, bring up the same old memories. It was good to know that Jim had a male friend in this world who really understood him.

After dinner, Jim went out and bought a bottle of Captain Morgan's Coconut Rum. It was Charlie's favorite. On the way home, Jim rolled down the windows in the truck while driving down the Overseas Highway He could not believe the beautiful evening. The air was thick with the warm summer moisture, yet it somehow felt cool in the soft moonlight. As he looked out Snake Creek Bridge, he could follow the moon to the horizon. The stars so bright, they reflected brightly across the water.

It reminded him of the night just before the last hurricane hit. With everything so peaceful, Jim got that gut feeling to batten down the hatches. It was always calmest on the water as winds clocked around just prior to a storm's arrival. He had only felt this feeling a few times in his lifetime, but each time the warning never went unanswered.

Later that same night Jim was tossing and turning. It was 2 in the morning when he had a recurring nightmare that had plagued him for many years.

Jim could still feel the cool of the water surrounding his body. The dive was going as planned. The Russian sub's escape hatch had been welded shut. Charlie was working on disabling the rudder. Jim and John were working on sealing the ballast intakes.

Unexpectedly, another diver appeared, just entering their limits of visibility at 30 feet. Recognizing the equipment, Jim realized in dread that this was not a friendly visitor, it was a Russian coming around the rear of the sub. Jim could only look up in horror as the Russian diver, who had somehow gotten out of the sub, assaulted Charlie quickly and viciously.

From a corner of Jim's eye, he witnessed as the Russian pulled out a large shiny knife and impaled Charlie in his left thigh. Jim instantly knew the diver to be exceptionally trained as he watched the Russian twist the knife to further open the wound. Then in one fluid motion, the Russian immediately cut Charlie's airline and he removed Charlie's mask.

With all his might Jim swam to his friend's aid. The stunned Charlie tried desperately fighting back terror and escaping his attacker's grasp. Reaching the Russian diver, Jim pulled off the attacker's mask. Jim was trained that on land you go for the nose, under water you go for the eyes. Before the attacker could react, Jim had reached around the adversary's head and with his thumb poked, then pulled out an eye from its socket.

Holding the Russian around the neck, he waited a moment for the cool salt water to hit the attacker's brain. Totally disoriented, the Russian started to convulse. Jim then pulled out his long K-Bar knife and brought the point home deeply in the attacker's chest. Twisting the knife, he waited as the body now became inanimate. He then let go and allowed the Russian to drift lifelessly toward the bottom.

With the main threat eliminated, he went back to Charlie's aid. Blood was everywhere in the water. John swam toward them and with hand signals they decided to get Charlie back into the sub.

John, however, insisted on being the sentry, just in case any other Russian divers were able to escape from a torpedo hatch or some other means. The moment seemed to hang for an eternity. Jim tried to call John back to the sub, but it was to no avail. Charlie needed medical attention; he was bleeding profusely. John refused the hand signals, he wanted to stay put.

Once back in the safety of the sub, Jim wanted to go back after John, but orders were to move fast. In the Seals, you were taught that you were a tool and that you were expendable. The mission was the first priority. Jim knew that John was doing what he had been trained and what was best for the team. He also knew that if anyone stood a chance at surviving, even as slim as the odds were, it would be John. Jim sat on the floor leaning against a bulkhead, dripping wet and tired from the adrenaline rush. He screamed, "Damn it, John!" as he pounded his fist on the cold unforgiving steel floor.

As the sub engaged propulsion and made its way out of the harbor, Jim's heart wrenched at leaving a follow warrior and such a good friend. What bothered him most was not being able to say goodbye.

Awaking in a cold sweat, Jim strained to focus on the red digital numbers displayed on the alarm clock on his nightstand. It was only 2:08 in the morning. Getting out of bed, he went to the kitchen, drank a glass of cold water, then headed back to bed. He hoped his demons would retreat and allow him the sleep he still so badly needed. It took nearly an hour, but eventually he drifted off to sleep.

When his alarm finally went off, his body wanted more rest, but it was time to start his day. Reluctantly he got up and began his morning ritual. Larry arrived on schedule and together they went to the docks.

The day's fishing was business as usual. Except for a really huge stray wahoo, the catch included the regular mix of dolphin, black fin tuna and an unusual summer sailfish. At the docks the boats all backed in side by side. All the captains and mates proudly displayed their catch while the usual happy hour crowd gathered to cheer each time that a really nice fish came out of a fish box.

After pictures and moneys were exchanged, the work began. Neatly filleting 40 to 50 fish was no easy task. Over the years Jim and Larry had perfected the skill. Before most people would have the skin peeled, Jim would have five cleaned and in the bag. It really was something to watch.

In most cases the passengers would donate fish to the crew. After the guest would leave, someone in the crowd would always want to buy fresh fish. In a few short minutes, the docks transformed into an outdoor fish market. It was an important way for captains and mates to supplement their income. They would then spend this money upstairs at the Harbor Bar, buying their friends drinks and swapping war stories about the day on the water.

Today he was displaying the large wahoo. Two local older women, wanting fresh fish for their family, started the biding process. When the bid hit 10 dollars, someone from behind them said, "Ten bucks, that fish must weigh 20 pounds, I'll give you 25." As if someone had broken a cardinal rule, the two old women turned in disgust and stared at this rule-breaker in the back of the crowd. Then, as if to not be out-done, the two women began the bidding process again. At $32.50, the woman on the left had bought her dinner.

From behind the crowd Charlie emerged grinning from ear to ear. "You are not really going to take that old woman's money, are you?" asked Charlie.

"Lady, what do you say you give me 15 bucks? I'll beat the other 20 bucks out of this big mouth here," as Jim pointed to Charlie, who was still grinning. The woman handed Jim the money, then carted off the fish. To her she had gotten the deal of a lifetime. Wahoo goes for $6.85 a pound at the Islamorada Fish House. She could barely manage carrying the large fish to her car.

"Boy, did you screw that up! You know, I would have gotten at least $30," said Jim to Charlie.

"She looked like she deserved a deal. Did you see the way she was fighting for that fish? She was a real scrap-per. Besides, where we're going, another twenty bucks isn't going to mean squat."

Brushing the seriousness of that remark aside, Jim turned to Larry, who was still cleaning up. "Hey, Larry, do you remember Charlie, my old running buddy?"

Larry said, "Who could forget that crazy Cuban, how ya been doing, Charlie. Jim says you're living in California. Welcome back to paradise!"

Larry turned and went back to scrubbing the coolers. Jim and Charlie headed up the steps leading to the Raw Bar. The setting was magnificent. As the sun was starting to reach the horizon, the hosts were on stage performing the Friday Night Radio Show.

The hosts would interview captains, letting locals and

tourist alike know what bite was hot on the water along with dive reports. They would also perform the community a great service by letting everyone know what events were coming up.

Charlie ordered Captain Morgan with a key lime. Kim the barmaid did not even have to ask Jim as she brought him the usual Dewar's on the rocks. "Who's your good-looking friend?" asked Kim.

"Charlie, may I introduce you to one of the finest people on this island. This is Kim."

Charlie's eyes sparkled as he reached out and took Kim's soft tan hand. "Nice to meet you," answered Charlie. Jim was like Kim's big brother. They had known each other for a long time. Kim was a rather tall girl of 29. She had long brown hair, a great skin color and green eyes. She was like a magnet to all males, both locals and tourists alike.

Every man who walked into the bar was easily attracted to her warmth and good looks. But try as they might, no one yet had been able to make her settle down. Kim went back to her other customers, but Jim noticed how the two of them kept glancing at each other. Jim thought they would make a good couple someday, if he could ever get him to slow down.

As Jim and Charlie talked, the miles and months between them began to fade. Before long they were both 20 years younger, laughing about the good memories and failing to bring up the disappointing ones. Larry walked in and sat down.

Jim knew how hard it was for Larry to even be in a bar, so before he could even order his usual club soda with a twist of lime, Jim said, "Linda's cooking tonight. If you guys are ready, let's head out."

Larry had lost his girlfriend eight years ago to a nasty head-on collision on the Seven Mile Bridge. They had spent the weekend at "Fantasy Fest" in Key West and were on their way back home late on a moonless Sunday night. Larry fell asleep at the wheel. For months he relived that night. All the things he should have, could have, would have done to change that day.

He finally decided to crawl into a bottle of Jack Daniel's, and it was only Jim who finally made him come out. But it was constant work. Larry would always tell Jim he was ready to drink again. Jim would have to talk him into waiting just a little bit longer. With a clear conscience, Jim could not drink around Larry in a bar, so they left and headed home.

Linda had a special Keys dinner ready for them when they arrived. Charlie thought it was the perfect way to start the mission that lay ahead. They started with conch fritters, then a main course of barbecued lobster tails, served with hot butter and garlic. For dessert they enjoyed the tart taste of Linda's homemade key lime pie. The meal and ambience was spectacular.

They ate on the verandah overlooking the picturesque Florida Bay. As they poured some more coffee and finished the last of the pie, only faint colors of the once-magnificent sunset could be seen toward the West. Like dying embers in a fading bonfire, another day was burnt into the history books of the Florida Keys.

With dinner cleared away, Jim asked Charlie, "Still enjoy a good cigar?"

"I could never turn down one from your stash, Jim."

The two got up and walked downstairs to the sea wall under his palm tree. With the stogies lit, all that could be heard was the far-off raspy, squawking cry of a blue heron calling to its mate. "So, let's get down to business, it's great to see you, but what the hell's up?" asked Jim.

"Jim, what I'm about to tell you is a Level One security, I need your word that regardless of whether you decide to help me or not, you will speak of this with no one, not even Linda." Charlie's usual fly-by-the-seat-of-his-pants smile was erased from his lips. He was stone cold, eyes letting Jim know this was no prank.

Jim was a little taken aback by Charlie even having to ask. Raising his hand in a Boy Scout sign, he answered, "You have my word, friend."

Charlie explained about his brother and about Basanta's nuclear program. They talked solemnly for many hours.

It was after midnight. The soft white sand around them looked like a stakeout from a Philip Marlow movie, with all the cigar butts smashed at their feet below them. Finally, Jim pointed to Scorpio sitting so bright in the Southern sky. Jim extended his finger down the body and through the tail. "You line up those last two stars on the tail and they point due south," he said as he extended his finger to the horizon. "Roughly a hundred miles that way, that's where we'll be by the end of the week."

"So are you in, Jim? Will you help us?" asked Charlie.

Jim nodded yes slowly with the look of a man who was risking everything he had for a friend.

"Jim, I feel terrible even asking you to go with me. I know when you got out, you always wanted to stay out, and I respect that. I thought long and hard about asking you, but it only makes sense. Hell, we've pulled off jobs tougher than this with our eyes closed. This time, however, if I screw up I could lose my brother. When it comes to this, you wrote most of the textbooks we still use for training. I sure would like to have you beside me when I go in there. You know the water, you know your boat, there is no one else I could trust."

"I'm proud to help out, Charlie; I was starting to get bored anyway." It was actually easier deciding to go than he had thought. The hard part would be not telling Linda the truth. Even with the growing void between them, she would not want him to go. He would tell her he was taking Charlie to the Bahamas for an extended fishing trip. If she knew the truth, one of the few remaining constants between them, his integrity, would be threatened.

"Jim, I didn't want to make this influence your thinking, but if we go in, we have a reunion of sorts awaiting us."

Jim looked at Charlie with a puzzled look.

"John Kelly," Charlie paused. "He is still alive! The bastards have had him all along. I just found out myself, but he is real close to where we will be."

"No shit, I knew he'd make it. Charlie, we've got to get his ass out of there."

"I know, but how? The damn place holds perhaps 200 political prisoners. My brother will try and locate his cell block, but the place is heavily armed." Pulling out a map and a floor plan of the prison, he spread it out before them.

"We have to take care of our main objective first. Then we'll have to set up a diversion and get John out," said Jim. "How much time do we have?"

"I plan on two hours max to work on John."

Using long mangrove seedpods like pencils in the sand, the two men spent several hours considering different strategies and approaches. After several long hours, they had three basic plans.

"You know me, Charlie, we have a basic plan, from there we'll have to wing it. You never know till we're standing in front of the damn place. We'll figure it out. Might be a little rusty, but we've always pulled it off before."

When the time came to turn in, Charlie asked if he could use the phone. Admiral Franklin would be waiting for the call. The admiral was pleased to hear that his old friend Jim had accepted the challenge. After hanging up with Charlie, he made the arrangements to have the supplies shipped in a Ryder truck from Homestead to Islamorada in the morning.

The next day started as usual with Larry driving up in his truck. "Larry, come on in here and sit down. Charlie and I need to talk with you." Charlie and Jim had decided that they could use Larry's help if he was willing to go with them. With security being so important, Charlie would not let Larry know until they were leaving exactly what they were doing. They all poured coffee and began talking it over.

"You mean, you want me to just hop on a boat and take off? I don't know where I am going or when I'll return, but I do know it's really important and I could be killed. It pisses me off, thinking that Charlie doesn't trust me enough to tell me, but if you need me, I'm there for you, Jim! You can count on me, God knows I've counted on you for the last couple of years."

"Terrific," said Charlie as he stood up and put his hands together as if praying and celebrating at the same time. "We'll have a boatload of gear to take on board. I don't think the crowd at Whale Harbor would understand our cargo too well."

"I don't think so," said Jim, "I do have the perfect spot, though, Port Bougainvillea. It is a development which was almost built. Environmentalists shut it down when they found an endangered rat living in the gumbo-limbo trees. Now all that remains is a ghost town with deep water access. Drug dealers have been using it for years."

"Sounds great. I'll call the truck, and we'll meet at 10 tomorrow," responded Charlie.

With plans for the voyage all set, Charlie used his digitally scrambled cell phone and called the com center in Florida City. He had already coded and sent them the message to be sent to his brother by the Nav-Fax. They awaited his authorization to send it.

The rest of the day was spent relaxing. They had a

charter with some tourist from Alabama. With only two passengers, Charlie went along as an observer. Jim did a lot of thinking during the day. When the day was over, Jim was convinced he was doing the right thing.

Before going to bed, Jim flipped on the TV. The rebroadcast of the news had Bryan Norcross giving the weather report. Jim didn't have much respect for most weather people; Brian was an exception. Brian was pointing to the Cape Verde Islands off of Africa. An ugly tropical wave had just turned into a tropical storm. Brian mentioned that it was nothing unusual, just something to watch.

As Jim rolled over to go to sleep, he reached over and took Linda's hand as he turned off the TV.

CHAPTER TWELVE

At 9 p.m., Captain Ricardo Balart switched on his fax machine and turned it to the proper frequency. Five minutes later, even with a towel placed over the machine to muffle the noise, a high-pitch noise could be heard, as the device went into receive mode and began printing. His pulse quickened as he knew what was coming across the fax, yet he calmly asked his crew if they had noticed a fire ball and pointed to the horizon. They quickly began checking the radar and used night vision scopes to try to ascertain what, if anything, had been seen.

With the transmission complete and the crew distracted, the captain discretely tore off the page and stuck it into his shirt pocket. Far off on the horizon another light erupted in what looked like a road map against the sky. With a laugh in his voice the lookout said, "It's only lightning, Captain, can we go back to work?"

"Si, I think I'll go below for awhile. Juan Carlos, you take the helm."

Ricardo resisted the urge to run to his cabin. Instead he walked calmly down the narrow metal corridor. With months of planing, this was the moment of truth. The message would either be a go or no-go. He nervously dropped his keys trying to open his cabin. Bending over to retrieve them, he felt his pulse beating in his temples.

Finally closing the door behind him, he turned on his light and retrieved the Ernest Hemingway novel. In just under 15 minutes Ricardo was putting the novel back on his shelf in his cabin. With the message decoded and read, he lit a match and placed the fax in the ashtray.

A warm smile appeared on the captain's face. Tomorrow the plan he had been working on for months would go into action. For his brother across the water, the ball was already rolling. With the last of the fax burning in the ashtray, Ricardo bent down as he always did and lit a cigar. As he leaned back and closed his eyes, he savored one last moment of peace as the bluish smoke filled the cabin and danced like a ghost before him.

In Cuba the good cigars get exported to black markets in America and wholesalers in Europe and Canada. Only the lesser-known brands or the rejects are available to the Cuban people. With his position, however, Ricardo was able to get the good stuff. The cigar he was smoking today sells for $20 US in Canada. It made Ricardo enjoy the aroma all the more.

With the gentle motion of the sea, Ricardo was almost asleep when there was a sudden knock on the door. "Captain, sorry to disturb you, but Commandant Gonzalez called and wants to talk with you immediately."

Ricardo quickly got to his feet and went to the bridge. On the way a yeoman traveling the opposite way down the hall had just made fresh coffee. "Want some coffee, Captain?" asked the yeoman.

The strong smell made Ricardo feel more alert. "I sure could use something, thanks," said Ricardo as he grabbed a shot of coffee. With the sweet, strong taste of the coffee he quickly felt refreshed and awake.

The call from his sergeant was just usual housekeeping reports. The most important piece of information was the scheduling of a week of down time for El Matador, beginning tomorrow. When the crew heard the news from the radio, an immediate but somewhat subdued cheer was heard by all. "Quiet, you guys, or instead of time off I'll get you assigned to other vessels," said the captain. Still smiling, the crew went back to their task at hand.

Three weeks ago, as part of the plan, Ricardo had tampered with the oil gauge on the port engine. By plugging up the gauge pick-up tube, it read as having low oil pressure. He even went as far as removing as much as five quarts of oil per night in order to make it appear the engine was burning excessive oil. He had scheduled the maintenance down time the previous week. Thank God his superior approved it, he thought. With the current state of disrepair his country was in, he wasn't so sure they would even fix her.

Ricardo's superior had instructed that both he and the helmsman were to take the ship to the maintenance facility at the mouth of the Mantanzas River, just to the west of Cardenas. The helmsman, Rolando Hernandez, had just been blessed with the birth of his fourth child. With the current workload of three kids, Rolando knew his wife would not be pleased when she found out he would be gone for a week.

This was the only piece of the puzzle Ricardo had not solved cleanly. If he had to take the helmsman, he would, but he was looking for a way out. Having to eliminate someone you have known for such a long time would be hard indeed. Knowing that Rolando's children would be without a father was heartbreaking, but Ricardo felt strongly about what he was doing. He knew going in that there would be tough choices and sacrifices. If Rolando would agree to stay behind, that would be best. If Rolando went, Ricardo would try to talk him into going along with the plan.

When they pulled back into port and were docked for the night, Ricardo waited until the rest of the crew had left. "Rolando, come in and sit down," instructed Ricardo. "Rolando, I understand your wife has just had another baby."

"Yes, Captain, another boy, one more soldier for the revolution," said Rolando.

Ricardo continued, "Rolando, as you know, I would very much like your help on the run to Mantanzas."

"Yes, Captain, I will be there," answered Rolando.

"I know that you would be a good soldier and go tomorrow, without complaint, but I have decided that you also can have the time off. I will take the vessel myself tomorrow. In honor of your dedication and good service, you deserve to spend a few days with your new son," said the captain.

"But Captain, how can you be expected to pilot and navigate such a large vessel by yourself?"

"I have done it so many times before, have no fear," the captain lied.

Rolando got out of his duty chair and stood up. With a serious look on his face he began to contemplate whether to follow his heart or follow his duty. He began to pace rather fast. Suddenly he stopped and said, "Captain, I would feel terrible if anything were to happen. My duty is first to the revolution and second to my family. I must go with you, Captain." It always amazed Ricardo how Latins communicated. What they say and what they mean are so different.

Captain Ricardo placed an arm around his helmsman and said, "Rolando, I'll be fine. Stay at home, keep a low profile, and I'll see you in a week."

"It will be as you command, Captain," said Rolando sternly.

A few moments later, Captain Balart was the only one left on the ship. As he watched his helmsman depart and begin to walk away, he could clearly see the jump and fist in the air, as the young man's exuberance could finally be freely displayed. Turning off the bridge lights, Captain Balart walked the empty corridors and left the ship.

Riding his bike home he began to take in the smells he would soon miss. After so many years of a routine, it was so easy to miss all the details. As he rode through the neighborhoods, the smells of Cuba permeated the thick night air. With no air conditioning everyone had their windows wide open. The whole city smelled like one big open air kitchen.

On one block he smelled his favorite meal being steamed. Black beans and rice would soon be served. He had heard that in America people eat early. Not so in Cuba. Here, people eat the largest meal right before going to bed. In the next block, the sizzling sounds and smells of green bananas being fried. His stomach began to grumble as he pedaled faster. Even with all he had on his mind, he was beginning to develop a voracious appetite.

As he turned onto the last street before arriving home, he heard a loud argument - or, as Cubans called them, discussions. The Ruiz family was at it again. With 12 people under one roof in this August heat, he was always amazed that violent crime was so low. But little by little, people were starting to get angry. You could only quell the rage so long. Ricardo wondered just how much longer Basanta's tether could keep his people oppressed. Once again his thoughts returned to the surreptitious mission that laid ahead.

As he arrived home and closed the door, Ana rushed to him. With one arm around his waist and the other on his shoulder, she kissed him, then leaned back and looked deeply in his dark eyes for the answer. For a moment Ricardo remained somber, then all at once his face began to glow; a huge smile came across his lips. Ana also began to smile. "So, it is all set?" asked Ana.

"Yes, we leave in the morning," said Ricardo.

Ana had spent the day packing feverishly. She could

only take a few small boxes. It was not what was to be packed that was difficult, but what was to be left behind. Ana was sentimental. Even after all these years, she still kept the first flower, or weed really, that Ricardo had picked in a field and gave to her back when they were still in school. Her small home was packed with memories. Ricardo was the opposite. Memories of the past could easily be discarded for the dreams of the future. For many years, Ricardo would sit up at night and tell Ana what life would someday be like, when they made it to America.

As Ana looked around, she began to cry as she realized that the plan was finally going to happen.

"Ana, I know it is hard. This is all you know. But trust me, we will do much better in America. "

"I know, Ricardo, but this is what we have. It may not be much, but it is all I know. When we leave, I don't have any guarantees, a lot can happen."

Being the adventurer at heart, Ricardo reminded Ana of the famous quote, "Ana, if Columbus never had the courage to lose sight of land, he would have never discovered the New World. Trust me, it will be all right." They finished packing and went to bed.

It had been many years since they had made love with so much passion and energy as they did on the eve of their departure. Channeling years of frustration, with the joy of knowing they were finally getting out, Ana screamed out powerfully as she rode on top of Ricardo.

When the lovemaking concluded, they were both soaked in sweet sweat wrapped in their sheets together. Dim candlelight gave the room a soft glow, as they faced each other, smiling in satisfaction and drifting off to sleep.

CHAPTER THIRTEEN

It was first light, 650 miles to the north of Mantanzas, Cuba. A Louisiana registered shrimp boat named Beulah Pride had just finished hauling in their trawl nets off Fernandina Beach, Fla., at the Georgia-Florida boarder. The crew was hard at work, dumping the night's meager catch on the main deck.

The crusty Cajun captain, Philip Debouis, said, "Da Gods mus be mad ot us fellas, luk's like 'nudda wasted night!"

Shrimping, like practically all forms of commercial fishing, was at most times a gamble. A captain had a hunch, talked with other captains and steamed off, sometimes hundreds of miles for what should have been more productive grounds.

Sometimes it would work, sometimes it didn't. Philip's favorite shrimping grounds were the seabeds off the Dry Tortugas, 68 miles west of Key West, Fla. Night after night, however, his catch began to progressively gross less tonnage. For a shrimp boat captain, that meant one thing: It was time to move on.

At night while dragging nets, he talked with other shrimp boats by short-wave radio, further up the Florida coast. They were raving about the catch off the mouth of the Saint John's river. In the hot August sun, the waters off Key West were in the 80s, and sometimes surface temperatures hit 92 degrees. It was assumed that perhaps cooler water to the north would be more productive. On intuition, he steamed north.

The Beulah Pride was one of eight boats owned by the Oyster Bay Shrimp Company, based in Chalmette, La. Beulah Pride was by no means the company's most modern vessel. Built of wood back in 1967, she was 68 feet of leaking, creaking timber.

Capt. Philip Debouis, like many other fishermen, liked wood over steel hull boats. At bars he argued with the other Cajun captains. He would say, "Da steel may be tuffur, but da vood floats. When da wader come in and che cannot stay aflut, I go fer da vood any tim." It was an argument that would never, and could never be, won. Every captain had his own preference.

The shrimping industry was dominated by Cajuns. They had a lifestyle and a way of communicating all to themselves. Listening to their chatter on their VHF channel, it was impossible to tell exactly what language they were speaking, much less what it was they were talking about.

It was a desolate life, to say the least. The crew would leave port and usually not return until their holds were full of quick frozen pink crustaceans. When things went great they could be back in a week. Usually, however, they would be gone for months at a time. Day in and day out, the boat was their home. Shipmates sometimes became the only family the crew members ever had.

The money could be good, and when the men hit port, they where usually paid in cash. Cash did not last long in the pockets of thirsty, tired and love-starved men, especially in a town like New Orleans. The money would usually pour through the bars quicker than the blood in their veins, long gone before it was even time to leave port again.

The culture they had was very similar to the nomadic carnival workers. For the most part, they were clan-like and kept to themselves. At sea, they depended on no outside help. When a shrimper got himself in a fix, he would rely on other shrimp boats to come to his aid.

They were one group that wanted nothing to do with the Coast Guard. Most likely, an encounter with the Coasties would mean an inspection. These old boats may be home to the shipmates, but most of the boats were patched together and kept afloat only by determination, luck and lots of hard work. With a lot of time on their hands, marijuana was a well-accepted pastime of most crews. Needless to say, a Coast Guard boarding was never a welcome event.

The crew on the Beulah Pride could never have been called a handsome lot. Months at sea had forced them to avoid many of the things that landlubbers took for granted. The only time a shrimper would visit a dentist, for example, would be when a tooth became so abscessed that even rum could no longer mask the pain.

At that point, too much infection had set in, and the only remedy would be to pull the tooth. Many times this dental procedure would be performed by another crew member on the high-rolling sea. Other times it would come from the unexpected fist of an ornery sailor at one of the rougher bars on the seedy side of Key West. They were five of the roughest-looking of men, all missing teeth, with leather like skin and unkempt hair.

Philip had been a shrimper as long as he could remember. His father had raised him while he ran the Beulah Pride. Back in 1982, Philip's dad died of a sudden heart attack in a whorehouse in Lafayette. Philip took pleasure knowing that at least he died doing something he enjoyed instead of going down in a late summer squall.

Philip had taken over after a long, hard tutelage from his dad. Capt. John Debouis had taught his son how to

81

keep the old girl afloat, even in the roughest of weather. Many nights, even years after his death, Philip had felt his dad's presence at the helm, especially in a storm.

Philip's brother-in-law, Jean Matisse, led the crew on this trip. Jean was a big, heavy Cajun. He had a red beard and arms as big around as telephone poles. Jean kept the others in line, and was in charge of maintenance on the vessel.

Pierre Bonnard was the cook, as well as an able-bodied deck hand. Pierre was skinny and almost sickly looking. His eyes were dark and rat-like, sunk deep into his forehead. Pierre was an incredible cook, and for that he was always popular aboard any boat. He was famous around the fleet for turning what appeared to be table scraps into a fabulous meal.

David Jacques-Louis was another Cajun. He had long dark hair, medium build, and was mostly a loner. He kept to himself and did what was told. David never started or encouraged conversation. People who worked with him figured he was a bit autistic. When it came to facts and figures he had a memory like a computer. Hard, physical labor was not David's forte; tedious work like gingerly sifting through 16 cubic yards of by-catch in order to find 100 pounds of shrimp was his thing. He would work without complaint for hours.

Clayton Jones was the only non-Cajun on the boat. He was a large barrel-chested man, pushing 300 pounds from Gulf Port, Miss. He was a black man and at age 38 he looked much older. Shrimping ran deep through his veins.

Clayton, or Clay as others knew him, had a laugh and a sense of humor that would keep you in stitches. Clay even mastered the Cajun language, mostly out of self-defense. If someone heard him and did not see him, even fellow Cajuns would swear he was one of their own.

With the morning sun rising, Clay and Pierre were busy tying off the netting, while Jean and David began the nasty, sweaty job of sorting through the by-catch. By-catch consisted of thousands of juvenile fish, blue and soft-shelled crabs, squid, eels, lobsters and just about everything else that inhabited the ocean floor. It amazed even them that it took 10 pounds of by-catch to produce a pound of shrimp for someone's dinner plate.

As if on cue, a huge school of black fin tuna and bonita commenced swirling in the calm morning water behind the boat. Crashing the surface of water, as if demanding their morning feeding. Looking over the rail, David took a shovel and tossed over a scoop of by-catch. The water instantly erupted in a feeding frenzy.

"Luk at dem damn fish, man," said Jean, pointing to the huge school devouring the tiny crabs and squids.

"Ya, at least sum goood cum out of dis trash," said Pierre from high up in the rigging.

The shrimp boats formed their own ecosystem. Towing nets, the Beulah Pride, could only move at one-and-a-half knots. Schools of fish would set up residence around the boat's perimeter. When the boat anchored in the morning, a wide variety of pelagic fish would instantly surface for breakfast. They grew to depend on the by-catch for survival.

Off the stern of the boat, blackfin and yellowfin tuna as well as many other kinds of fresh fish, were caught almost daily, supplementing the crew's evening meals. Shrimpers, however, tired easily of fresh fish, lobster and jumbo shrimp and dreamt of a warm greasy quarter-pounder with cheese and large fries.

The Beulah Pride, being an older boat, was slow moving at work. She had two 50-foot-wide nets that were spread by a beam and a sled with an otter door. The sled would rake the bottom and would push the nets deep and to opposite sides of the boat. Philip planned on replacing the doors with a newer, faster system that would allow her to double her speed.

For the next several hours the brutal work in another day in the life of a shrimper took place. The entire crew, with the exception of Captain Philip, sorted through trash. They filled large green mesh bags with shrimp and took them below to quick freeze.

The Beulah Pride may not have been a beautiful ship on the outside, but in her hold she had a state-of-the-art refrigeration system. They employed a method of freezing called IQF. IQF stood for Individually Quick Frozen, a process that individually froze each shrimp as soon as it was stored. This allowed shrimp to be sorted and shipped individually instead of large lots.

At 9:20 a.m., a center console fishing boat sheepishly pulled up behind the Beulah Pride. The boat was a 28-foot White Water, built down in Miami. They were obviously heading out for a day's fishing. Fishing rods were placed in rod holders from every conceivable place on the skiff.

When they were within shouting range, a man on the bow of the small boat yelled up, "Y'all got any trash?"

Clay yelled back, "What you boys have to trade for?"

"We have us some ice cold Budweiser," answered the fisherman.

Cold Bud was a staple of shrimpers. Most fishermen heading out would always pick up a case of the stuff in hopes of trading for by-catch. They would not want to take a chance with any other kind of beer. For some reason even men at sea could be picky.

"Got any joints?" howled Pierre.

"No sir, not us, just some beer," said the fisherman.

"How many buckets ya want, boys?" asked David, standing next to a mountain of trash.

"Three buckets should get us by," said the driver of the skiff, not wanting to sound greedy.

They slowly transferred the trash that would soon be

chum for the fisherman. At least a little more by-catch did not go to waste, thought David.

As the small boat moved out and headed to sea, the crew of the Beulah Pride began shoveling the rest of the trash out of the scrubbers on the side of the deck. The scrubbers could be closed, but were usually left open. They were simply holes, cut at the deck line in the gunnel's, or ship's, sides. They allowed sea water that came over the side in a storm to leave the deck and pour back into the ocean. They also functioned as a convenient way to get rid of the by-catch.

With the decks once again clean and the nets raised just above the water, Jean went in and woke up the captain. Captain Philip had been catching some rest while the crew worked through the morning.

"Well, Jean, time to pull da anchor. Tim to head bak south," said Captain Philip.

With a hold only halfway filled with shrimp, the weary, frustrated crew pulled anchor and set course back to the Dry Tortugas. They had decided to return to their favorite spot. It was late in the season. They would give the Keys one last try and then make their way back to Louisana It would soon become the single worst error in judgment Captain Philip ever made.

CHAPTER FOURTEEN

Ernesto Gonzalez was the type of person one would easily look at in a crowded room and really not see. He was 5 feet 6, he had hair shaved close to his scalp, he was in his late 50s and wore large oval-shaped glasses.

Ernesto lived in the past. His apartment in Cardenas, Cuba, was full of antiquities of a time long gone. He was meticulously groomed; his nails were trimmed and manicured. He even went as far as plucking excess eyebrow hairs, especially on the bridge of his nose.

As he got up from his overstuffed red lounge chair, he went to his record player. It was an old RCA. He began flipping through his record collection. Finally, a smile came across his face and he removed one of his favorites, the Pasa Doble, played by Arturo Montero, from Valencia. It made no difference to Ernesto that the record was from 1952. As it began playing, he felt like it was only yesterday.

Yesterday was a time when he was respected. A time when he was young and everything in his world was right. His mother was alive then. They used to dance to this very song. To him no woman he had ever met had lived up to his mother. In his mother's eyes, he was always right. She had loved him so.

That's probably why Ernesto had discovered after many years that he was homosexual. Sure, he had dated women. He had even brought them home to meet his mother. She would have none of them. She would always find fault. They were too fat or too skinny; no one would ever please her. After many years he secretly turned to men. This was his greatest secret. Even his own mother would never suspect Ernesto was gay. With his stature in the communist party, certainly he would be destroyed if it ever came out. He felt a tinge of terror and at the same time a great deal of satisfaction, just thinking about it.

As the scratchy song ended, so did his memories. He looked at his watch; it was 11:45 p.m. Most in the town of Cardenas was already in bed. Not Ernesto, he had to go back into his lab and check on the 6 p.m. experiment. The results should have been ready. He quickly got dressed and left his apartment.

The walk to Nautilus Project was short. Only two blocks down a damp narrow cobbled street. He ascended wooden stairs and turned on the lights. As he looked around the room, a tremendous feeling of power engulfed him. This was a feeling he had not felt for many years. Within the confines of this small room was the awesome power of nuclear energy. From the outside no one could ever suspect.

Ernesto liked the feeling of superiority. It gave him power knowing he could kill millions of people at the drop of a switch. In the pit of his stomach, though, he knew that he did not possess the intestinal fortitude. He really did not want to hurt anyone but only wanted respect.

It was only pure luck that led him to his theory. One night while studying at the university, he had this idea. He came across a formula to extract pure plutonium from nuclear waste. After three years of testing, it appeared to work. He remembered his first meeting with Basanta. He remembered Adolfo's sheepish grin. Overnight he went from being a nobody to being one of the country's leading scientists.

Anything he wanted, he could get. Snickers bars were his favorite. No one in Cuba could get them, yet he had bags and bags of them stashed in his freezer. It was more power than anyone in his family had ever had. One piece of good advice he had received from an ex-lover had also paid off. All too often, one's pride makes one want to share secrets with the world. Ernesto had been disciplined enough to refrain. He never wrote anything of consequence down. In the laboratory, he kept volumes of totally fictitious records. He possessed photographic memory. He used this to his advantage. If he were to fail, so would the Nautilus Project.

At first Basanta did not like this, but soon he became complacent. The major in charge of the project gave assurances to Basanta that he would personally see to it that the mission succeeded. In outward appearances, it would seem to be an unimportant project. Upon closer inspection, though, the true scope would be seen.

The entire building had been commandeered for the project. It was an old cigar factory before the revolution. There was a team of five crack security personnel assigned to this office. No one could enter or exit without being identified. If a stranger did happen by, he would quickly be taken down in the fashion all too often seen in Cuba.

Cuba's chief of intelligence, Major Javier Suarez, was directly in charge of the project. He kept a long, but firm arm on Ernesto. Most of the time Ernesto had no idea he was being watched. In fact, he was in a fish bowl, being recorded and photographed at will.

His nuclear experiments were contained in what used to be a large vault in the factory. As he turned the tumblers and opened the heavy steel door, a buzzer went off on the security panel. The guard on duty quickly switched on the surveillance camera to the vault. Hitting the speed dial number on the phone in front of him, he called Major Javier Suarez.

The major was 57. He was taller than most of his Cuban comrades at 5 feet 11. He was trim and in generally good physical shape. His dark black hair and dull brown eyes, however, gave him a sinister look. He looked like someone who could take pleasure in watching others suffer. As a young man, he had been part of the revolution. To make him look even more evil, a 3-inch scar, courtesy of a bayonet wound, ran from just under his pointy chin up the left side of his lips.

With Cuba trying desperately to re-establish itself as an international tourist destination, a small cellular network had been set up last year. Although it rarely worked, it was the rage of anyone with power in Cuba.

Sitting in a café on the East Side of Havana, Javier's cellular phone rang loudly. Reaching in his coat pocket, he took out a flip-out Motorola and answered it in a deep raspy voice, "Diga me (Tell me)."

"Major, Ernesto is at work again. We have not been able to determine on our own if yesterday's experiment was a success," said the guard on duty.

"I want you to record every move that queer makes," said Javier. "Let me know how he reacts when he reviews the test results. If he so much as farts, I want a video of it on my desk tomorrow." Without even saying goodbye, he looked down and with a loud clap closed the flip phone. Sliding it back in his pocket, he went back to eating his meal of garlic-soaked lachon (roast pork) with black beans and rice.

Ernesto was a hard one to figure out. Exuberant or sad, he would always have the same bland look on his face. Interpreting these emotions became a great challenge to the people assigned to watching him. As he peered at the test results, he placed his hand to his chin. To those watching this bellwether, his actions became known as a good sign. To himself he thought, "Damn, it just is not working." With all the equipment, he had yet to perfect the process on a large enough scale to produce the amount of enriched pure plutonium needed for a single weapon. He was missing something. It had to be obvious. He sat down on the floor and began playing the entire process through his mind, from the beginning to the end.

The basic process was actually quite simple. He had found an unusual bacteria from the Brazilian Rain Forest that thrived on waste uranium. As the bacteria eat off the waste uranium, what is left is pure enriched uranium or U-235 plutonium. The problem is the bacteria dies off long before enough plutonium U-235 is harvested to make a weapon. The bacteria thrive in a tannic caustic solution when fed a steady supply of waste uranium. What causes them to die off after only a few hours?

He got up and looked up some old test results. Without writing down anything he made a mental note and began to compare his results today. For an hour he continued to do this. In infinitesimal amounts the process worked completely. What was he missing? He began to frown. Perhaps it will not work, perhaps it will never work. This wall he had run into now seemed insurmountable.

All at once a smile came across his face. The security man saw this and quickly zoomed in on him. He rose to his feet and left the room momentarily and returned with a small cup of coffee and a Snickers bar. The security man put down his head on his hands in frustration. During this moment, with the camera focused on the cup of coffee, Ernesto walked across the room and made a slight adjustment to the tannic acid formula. With the same blank look on his face he picked up his coffee, turned off the lights and pushed hard on the heavy steel door. With a slight smile, he spun the combination wheel and began to leave the room.

The security man switched the camera to the hall and then the stairwell as he followed him out the main door. As Ernesto walked home, he felt a feeling of confidence he had not felt before. This was it, he thought. He had found the answer. In the morning he should know if it had worked. It would be difficult for him to sleep tonight. The street was damp and quiet as he made his way back to his apartment. In his right pocket he removed the half-eaten Snickers bar, opened it and placed it in his mouth. With a smile he entered his apartment and got undressed.

CHAPTER FIFTEEN

I t was 5:10 in the morning as Jim fired up the port engine. After all these years, Jim still enjoyed the excitement of an early-morning adventure and the distinct smell of diesel fuel. With the port engine running, he started the starboard. As soon as they both reached the proper temperature, Larry removed the dock lines, and they were under way. Jim smiled. What would his buddies at the dock think when they arrived and found him long gone?

The morning was still. Far to the east, the colorful beginnings of another day slightly revealed themselves. The run to Key Largo took just under 45 minutes. Using his GPS and chart plotter, Jim found the unmarked channel and entered Point Bougainvilla. As they made their way through the canals, they reached the position for the transfer. Jim expertly backed his boat into a slip, which allowed the best access to the remnants of a parking lot.

As Charlie looked around, he became a little spooked. The place reminded him of a ghost town. Except for the palm trees and water, he felt like he was back in the Amazon. It was hard to imagine this in Florida. As he looked around, he was amazed at just how quickly the tropical foliage once again regained its dominance. It was obvious the entire place would, in a matter of years, be engulfed by vines and trees.

Architecturally the place was designed beautifully. Condos and townhouses built with a tropical flair lined the canals. Some had windows, others even had drywall already installed. He could just imagine the bankers' faces. All the bulldozers stopped because of an endangered rat. As Charlie helped tie a dock line, a large, startled green iguana scurried from behind the piling.

The roar of several vehicles quickly changed the absurd quiet of the deserted development. Brakes squealed as the glare of bright headlights could be seen behind the boat. There was one bright yellow Ryder truck and a government vehicle. The car did not say government, but the large black wall tires with tiny hub cabs all but gave them away. The truck was full of supplies, the car full of soldiers.

As if they had somehow followed the vehicles' exhaust vapor trail, a swarm of tiny black mosquitoes began to buzz around everyone's faces. "Now I really feel like we're in the jungle," said Larry as he slapped at a pair of mosquitoes both impolitely sucking blood from different sections of his shoulders.

In the Keys, you rarely encounter mosquitoes in great numbers. The Mosquito Department sprays for them around the clock in the summer. In this unpopulated area, they were free to breed in all the tiny puddles of water collected in deserted construction materials.

Lieutenant Balart read the sergeant's orders judiciously, then greeted the team from Homestead. In a matter of moments, a line of three men and one woman was formed, and the equipment was transferred to the vessel. With the gear loaded and signed for, the vehicles left as quickly as they had arrived.

Looking at Larry, Jim witnessed the stunned and bewildered look on his face. Larry had heard of SAM's and seen pictures of the AK47 automatic machine guns, but had never seen them in person. As he picked up a box of C4 explosives, the reality was beginning to set in. For the most part, all the weapons and gear they would take into Cuba were Russian-built weapons. In typical Navy Seal tradition, they would not want to leave any evidence that an American had ever been there. Jim wasted no time as he fired up his diesels, pulled the dock lines and put the boat in gear.

As the boat left the canal, and the depth beneath the stern gradually registered 5 feet, Jim hit the throttles which brought the Mystic Lady on plane. With the lines all stored, Larry climbed to the bridge and asked Jim, "What the hell is going on and where are we going?"

Sensing the slight panic in Larry's tone, Charlie said, "Come down below, I'll go over everything." As the two crew members left Jim alone, he plotted his course and set the auto pilot for Cay Sal Bank, Bahamas. Once entered, he sat back in his seat. With the long ride ahead, he tried to relax, but with all he had to loose, fear was his only companion as he sat alone on the bridge.

As they crossed the reef line, Jim could make out a smaller vessel in the distance. By now the sun had started to rise, and with the exception of a dark thunderstorm far to the Northeast, it would be another fine day. With modicum light, it was difficult to see, but from the shape of the tower, the vessel directly on his heading looked like the Semper Fi out of Venetian Shores. He adjusted his autopilot in order to cross well astern of the other vessel. He knew his friend Sarge, a former Marine, would be looking forward in search of birds.

The morning was always Jim's favorite time. Today, even though he felt he was heading into battle, it was no exception. With a hot cup of black Java in one hand and a pair of binoculars in the other, Jim took a deep breath inhaling the cool yet salty morning air.

Just as he was beginning to relax, he saw another vessel approaching off his port bow. Figuring it to be just another cargo ship he put his Steiner binoculars down until he was closer. The sky almost appeared to be magical at that time of the morning. Not really dark, yet not really light, it was a filtered world that made it difficult to see. The heavens around them were engulfed in a hue of soft pale blues.

They were cruising fast now at 24 knots, three-quarters throttle for the Mystic Lady. Jim was sitting above the cabin on the fly bridge. Eight feet below, Larry and Charlie both came out of the cabin. Charlie's briefing had taken some time. For a tense moment Jim looked down from the bridge at Larry. Larry just stood there with a serious look on his face. Then suddenly, a smile began to creep across Larry' s face, and he gave Jim the thumbs-up sign.

"Sure am glad you're with us, Lare, hate like hell to leave your ass out here if you decided not to go," said Jim with a smile.

Jim went back to the lookout as both Larry and Charlie climbed the ladder up to the bridge. Jim could make out the ship better now. "Oh, crap," said Jim as he looked from the binoculars. Charlie and Jim looked to see a medium-sized ship at "CBDR", constant bearing decreasing range, in other words on a possible collision course. At first it looked like only a fast freighter, then after another minute even Charlie could make out the distinctive orange of the Coast Guard markings on the ship's side.

Jim had the right of way. Altering course, even slightly, might have appeared like he was trying to inauspiciously avoid contact. Jim could try and hail the other vessel on

Florida

West Palm

Miami

Islamorada

Key West

The Straights of Florida

Elbow Cays
Lighthouse

Cay Sal Bank

Bahamas

Anguilla
Cays

Havana   Cardenas

Cayo Coco

CUBA

Peninsula De Zapata

the VHF radio, but he decided to stay put and see what happened. If it looked like they were actually trying to intercept, he would be forced to make a course change.

Making a bead directly for the Mystic Lady, the distance to target incessantly decreased on the radar screen. Jim had to hold back natural instincts that told him to spin the wheel in another direction and vacate the area while they still had time.

"Let's put out some baits, Lar. If we are engaged in fishing, sudden moves would look much more natural and we would be less likely to be boarded," said Jim.

Playing a high-stakes game of chicken, Jim lowered the outriggers into place from the bridge. Larry set out three lines with artificial lures.

With the distance to target at six-tenths of a mile, the Coastie finally altered course and passed well to the stern of their vessel.

"Never thought we'd be trying to make ourselves invisible from our own guys," said Larry.

"Yeah, remember we're the good guys, Charlie. Can't our boys in Washington at least give us a get out of jail free card or something!" said Jim.

Charlie said, "I wish it were that easy, guys. Our friends in Washington would not even remember our names if our cover got blown. We're breaking every international law known in the books to make this baby work. The only thing they did do for us was get us phony Bahamian customs documents. They state that we are on a fishing trip from Florida and that we cleared customs in Bimini," said Charlie.

"I brought the Bahamian Courtesy Flag. But I don't think they'd understand all the fishing gear," said Jim.

What none of the crew realized was that they did indeed have a friend. Admiral Franklin had a transponder on board. Every second the position, speed and direction was transmitted via satellite to a computer in the admiral's office. At his disposal the admiral had the alpha class submarine USS Baltimore making lazy S turns in the Florida Straits, never more than 15 nautical miles from the Mystic Lady as she made her crossing. Two F18 fighters were on standby alert at Homestead Air Force Base.

It was now 10:30 a.m. and Larry asked, "You guys want some breakfast? I'm starving."

The rapid beat of Jim's pulse had finally slowed down to a more normal tempo. He was feeling more confident and was ready for a good meal. "Sure, Larry, I'll have one of your mystic omelets."

"Mystic omelet, sounds great. What do you put in it?" asked Charlie.

"Whatever I find," said Larry. " Jim, did we use all that squid for bait yesterday?"

"Yeah, too bad, but there are those nice lobster tails I brought along in the fridge."

Larry was actually quite a cook. He used the lobster along with peppers and onion to make a spectacular omelet. Along with crisp hash browns and toast, they relaxed and enjoyed a good meal.

After several hours of running, Larry scanned the gauges. He wished he had cleaned out the port engine heat exchangers before leaving. The port engine was running 13 degrees hot. With 18 miles left, they should be OK. He would work on it when they hit Cay Sal.

Cay Sal is only a tiny spit of land located between the Bahamas Bank and Cuba. It is known for very strong currents and rough seas. The raging Gulf Stream currents try to overcome this speed bump called Cay Sal, in its path. The islands were uninhabited. A solitary lighthouse, warning seafarers what lurked in the jagged teeth of the reefs that encircle the small island marked it. Inside the lighthouse there is always a storeroom filled with food and water from past "Balsaros," or Cuban rafters, who had been rescued. The closest Bahamian Island to Cuba, Cay Sal has long been a stopping point for rafters on their trek to Florida.

As Jim continued to follow his auto pilot, he silently grew concerned. In his gut he felt he should not be steering as far to the southeast. He began to doubt the direction his GPS unit was telling him to steer. He hoped he had earlier correctly entered the coordinates in the machine. As a rule, when you are totally disorientated, and you begin to loose faith in all your navigation equipment, this is the time to trust them the most.

Jim remembered many other times when his course to steer home just didn't feel right. He felt he should be steering in a different direction. He remembered how he would relax and trust the GPS. It had never failed him. When he would reach port he would always be amazed by just how much that old Gulf Stream current had faked him out.

After several more tense minutes of scanning, finally far on the horizon, what looked to be a lighthouse appeared in the binoculars. As much has Jim had faith in his modern electronics, it was always good to have a visual on your destination. As they moved even closer, Charlie came back up on deck. Before him, in his future, lay his past. On this tiny rocky outpost, Charlie would hopefully see his long-lost brother.

Jim tried the different weather frequencies on his VHF radio. Finally he found a half-decent signal from the weather station in Key West. It was no real cause for alarm, but TD4, tropical depression number four of the season, had intensified. It had reached tropical storm strength with sustained winds of 55 miles per hour. The National Hurricane Center gave it the name Diana. It was moving west at 19 miles per hour, a good clip for a storm.

Jim had hoped it would slow down. Right now it was only a danger to ships at sea. It would not be expected to make landfall in the Eastern Caribbean for another three to four days. They should be back home by then.

As the depth of the water rose from 2,000 feet to around 90 feet, right before the reef, the colors abruptly changed. The deep cerulean color of the Gulf Stream was replaced by the powder blue of the sand being reflected off the bottom in the translucent water. As Jim carefully maneuvered the boat through the safest passage over the reef, Charlie and Larry took in the beauty of the pristine shallow reef.

Soon after crossing the reef, a huge, spotted eagle ray crossed their bow. It was followed by what appeared to be several large cobias. It killed Jim not to toss a bait to the huge cobia, but he knew they could not risk being spotted.

"Not making it easy for you to find your way to the hole with no markers?" said Larry with a chuckle.

The absence of channel markers, guiding them in, was a little unnerving. In the States they had it much easier. That alone emphasized to them just how remote and desolate a location they had come to.

"Makes it tricky, but the water is so clear I can see the channel fine," answered Jim.

Just before ducking into the hurricane hole, a cove on the northeast corner of the island, Jim backed off the engines. As the boat sat down off plane in the water, Jim began a thorough search of the horizon. With no vessels in sight, he slowly slid into the peaceful protection of the cove.

Once in the cove, Jim picked as deep a spot as he could find to anchor. He was not sure whether it was high or low tide and wanted as much of a safety margin as possible. Without a word spoken, Larry made his way to the bow and set out the anchor.

" 'Bout 12 feet under the keel. Let's set out two anchors off the bow and one off the stern," said Jim.

"I'll set out about 85 feet of line to have 7-to-1 scope," replied Larry.

"Should hold us fine, Larry," said Jim.

With the anchor set, Larry cranked on the generator and turned on the air conditioning. After the long ride and hot sun, it would be great to take a cool shower and grab some much-needed sleep. With the scorching afternoon sun overhead, the crew headed below after their thankfully uneventful crossing.

Jim headed for the engine room with his trusty old tool box. As Jim removed the cover to the raw water strainer, used to filter water to the heat exchanger, he immediately grew concerned. He expected to find it clogged with seaweed, but with the exception of an insignificant amount of grass, it was clean. He began to feel a knot in the pit of his stomach as he began to tear down the rest of the cooling system.

CHAPTER SIXTEEN

The night had been tough for both Ana and Ricardo Balart. It was the last night they both would sleep in the only country they had ever known. At 3:45 a.m., after tossing and turning, they both decided it would be better to just get up and get an early start. They loaded the few bags of memories they could take on their cart and attached the cart to the back of a bike.

The ride was peaceful as they pedaled down the pre-dawn street. Except for two cats fighting on a porch, the only sounds they heard were the squeaks and clanks from the tired old bicycle they were riding. It was a strange feeling, sneaking out of a place that for so long had been home. In a way, they felt like children sneaking out of their window at night for a round of mischief. If they were caught tonight the consequences would be much more severe. Only one more trip, thought Ricardo. Cautiously they pedaled the final blocks to the shipyard.

As planned, no one was around as they quickly loaded their belongings and boarded El Matador. Above in the tropical sky, an exceptionally large moon illuminated their passage. In just a couple of hours the dock would be bustling, but as they started the engines and untied the dock lines only eerie silence enveloped El Matador.

The ride had taken forever. Instead of setting a course directly for Cay Sal, Ricardo had decided it would be safer to cruise the coast. As he followed his usual patrol area, Ana was able to come up to the bridge. For the first time ever, she had been able to look around the vessel and realize the responsibility her husband carried with his position.

After a four-hour run along the coast, and with the shortest amount of open ocean to cross, Ricardo set a course directly for Cay Sal. It was a half-hour before they finally lost sight of Cuba. Ana looked back. A tear formed in the duct of her eye. Ricardo put his arm around her and gave her a reassuring hug. "It'll be all right, Ana."

"I know, Ricky, but this is all I know. Good or bad, at least I knew Cuba's bad habits. I knew what to expect," said Ana.

Ricardo tried reassuring her, "Just wait, Ana, just wait, and you'll never look back again." With the sun beginning to rise on their right, they continued their journey into the unknown. The glow in the sky above Cuba began to fade quickly with the dawn of a new day.

As usual, the seas picked up during the crossing. The wind was from the northwest at 12 miles per hour, kicking the seas up to a modest 4 feet. Not a lot of wind, but it was blowing in the opposite direction of the current. In this large vessel, the seas were only an unrelenting chop and of no real consequence.

In another hour, the Cay Sal lighthouse came into view. Ricardo's pulse quickened. He could feel the excitement of soon being reunited with his brother. He began studying his chart on the table in front of him. He had earlier marked the best place to cross the reef. It would be close, but, according to his tide tables, he should clear the razor-sharp reef by a comfortable 3 feet.

As he silently slipped into the hurricane hole and first caught sight of Mystic Lady, his heart was heavy with emotion. Larry, who was up on the deck, would not soon forget the sight of the gray Cuban war ship entering their safe little cove. His first feeling was one of apprehension. What if they had been found out? What if this was the bad guys? His uneasiness was quickly replaced by jubilance as he saw Ricardo and Ana waving from the open bridge window.

It was not easy to maneuver the large vessel alongside the smaller fishing boat. It took Ricardo several tense moments before he was in place and ready to drop anchor beside his American friend. Larry had tied lines into a monkey fist and along with four dock bumpers he quickly rafted the two vessels together.

Jim heard the rumbling noise of the other ship's diesels and came up from the engine room. Covered in grease, he in no way looked like the captain. Charlie's exuberance could not be controlled. The big, tough guy welled up in tears. As soon as the boat could be boarded, he leaped on the deck and made his way for the bridge.

The miles and the years quickly melted away as the two brothers embraced each another. Ana just beamed as she witnessed the long-lost brothers together at last. "Charlie, this is my wife, Ana. Ana, this is my brother, Charlie," said Ricardo in Spanish. As the three took each other in, Jim and Larry made their way to the bridge of the Cuban vessel. For both of the brothers, the anticipation they felt was well worth the wait as they celebrated and laughed.

After a brief introduction, Jim went back to his own engine room. Larry and Charlie began the transfer of equipment to the Cuban boat.

"Sure seems like a lot of equipment for just one day in Cuba," said Larry.

"I always try to cover all the bases and plan for every

situation. You just never know what we might be up against. Hell, I could blow up helicopters, or even tanks, if I have to. Better safe than sorry," said Charlie.

Ricardo guided the men to his quarters, where they carefully stored the majority of their supplies.

With the equipment transferred, it was time for a refreshing swim. Taking off his shirt, Larry dove off the transom.

"Ricardo, hand me my dive mask and fins, please. I'll also need my Hawaiian Sling. Let's see how fast I can catch us some dinner."

Compared to the reefs off Islamorada, the reefs of Cay Sal looked to be from another planet. Untouched beauty surrounded Larry he slowly stalked his prey. Queen Conch, once plentiful in the Keys and now almost extinct, were everywhere in the crystal-clear waters of the lagoon.

Ricardo and Charlie also jumped in and enjoyed the cool refreshing water of the harbor. The clarity of the water was breathtaking. As the three men snorkeled, they could see clearly across the lagoon. Each armed with a spear gun, they combed the clear blue water surrounding the boats. In a matter of minutes, fresh snapper and 10 large lobsters were tossed on the deck of the smaller boat.

CHAPTER SEVENTEEN

Jim had been down below in the engine room. The sweltering heat made him saturated in sweat; he deserved some good news. As he continued to trace his overheating problem, he had finally decided to pull the water pump.

With the final bolt removed, a few light taps with a small hammer and the thin paper gasket broke loose. As the water pump came away from the engine and green coolant spilled into the bilge, Jim gasped and his heart sank. Of the five steel impellers on the pump, only three remained; the other two had broken off and were missing.

He had always prided himself on the ability to fix anything on his boat by improvising. This time, however, without an arc welder, he was stumped. All he could do was put it back together, cuss out loud, and hope for the best.

As Jim got back on deck, even the warm tropical air felt cool across his sweaty skin in the light breeze. Jim took off his soaked shirt and also dove into the cool, clear water. It was refreshing, as he swam away from the boat. After a nice long swim around the lagoon, he returned to the boat. He still was concerned about the water pump, but he was much more relaxed. He had decided that as long as they did not push it, they should be able to make the crossing home without the engine overheating enough to cause a catastrophic failure.

With a beautiful sunset drenching the sky above them, it was easy to forget that they were on a mission. The five enjoyed a wonderful meal on the aft deck of the Mystic Lady. Larry, being the cook at heart, prepared the feast. This was one of the best Jim could remember. As they finished the meal, Jim poured what was left of a bottle of wine, Spanish Rioja. The dinner was awkward for Larry. He did a lot of nodding and smiling, as most of the conversation was in Spanish. Larry could not believe how well Jim got by in Spanish.

"If we leave at 3 in the morning, we should reach the Mantanzas Maintenance Facility by 6," said Jim.

"I think we should leave at 2, at 6 people may already be starting to stir," said Ricardo.

Jim said, "Very well then, at 2; we will leave then." Jim and Larry agreed to keep watch through the night and let Charlie and Ricardo get some much-needed rest.

Charlie set up shop in a cabin on the fore deck of the Cuban ship. He spread out all the satellite images and compared them to the antiquated maps he had been supplied. Ricardo joined him as they went over Charlie's plans carefully. They would enter through a window on the second floor. It would be well secured and they would have to compromise somewhat sophisticated security.

Unfortunately, they had no way of knowing just how secured the laboratory would be. After checking the equipment and feeling somewhat relieved, they sent the pre-coded Navfax, with the all-ahead green message. They also included their departure time.

Admiral Franklin received the call at 11 o'clock. "Are you nuts, the mission is green?" the admiral screamed into the phone. "Do they know that Hurricane Diana has reached 120 mph and is heading for Antigua?"

"No, sir, well, I don't know, sir. I will try to fax them, sir," said Petty Officer John Alderson on duty at the Communications Center at the Mayport Naval Air Station.

"You do that, son, then you get back to me when you hear something. Get a message off to Captain James on the USS Baltimore, tell him to keep a close watch on our boys."

For the next several hours, Alderson continued trying to reach the Navfax on the Mystic Lady. Unfortunately, in an effort to be secure, the machine had been turned off immediately after their transmission had been sent. Jim was on watch as the air began to cool in the starry, tropical night. Jim sat up in his tower in order to get the best look around.

Amongst the presence of typical small puffy clouds, the view was breathtaking in the soft yellow light from the moon. From time to time he would turn on his marine radio. He would scan the channels and try the weather frequencies. Even with the clear night, the signal from Key West was nothing but dead air. Nothing but static could be heard.

Jim never liked making the crossing blindly, but he figured that this time he had no choice. It was late; his Rolex said 11:58 p.m. He yawned and stretched when he heard a noise below. "Still awake up there, boss," said Larry.

"Yeah, but I sure could use some sleep," answered Jim.

"Relief is on its way," said Larry as he made his way up the ladder. Jim and Larry sat there for a moment. They took in the night around them, and Larry asked Jim, "Worried about tomorrow?"

"Sure, you always worry, but I think we will be just

fine. Charlie is a regular guerrilla. Together we make a hell of a team," said Jim.

"I hope so. This timing thing scares the hell out of me. You want me to wait 14 hours and if you don't show, head north? Jim, that would be a tough call."

"I know, buddy, but you have to do it. Don't worry, we'll make it back with time to spare," answered Jim. With that said, he climbed down the ladder and went to his cabin for an hour of shuteye.

He could barely get undressed before he was beginning to feel his body scream for sleep. The day had been long; his body needed rest. The quick-flowing adrenaline that had been pumping in his veins had robbed him of energy. As the boat gently creaked, he drifted off into a deep sleep.

CHAPTER EIGHTEEN

E arlier that same evening of August 13, the Cuban president was looking rather dapper, dressed in a tuxedo instead of his usual olive drab uniform. He had decreed a birthday celebration for himself along with a group of his high-ranking officials. In a corner of the hall, a band was playing soothing salsa music.

The president smiled as he put his arm around his good friend Major Suarez, the director of intelligence, and asked, "So, my friend, how is our good doctor Ernesto doing? Is Nautilus Project on schedule?"

Suarez felt a slight tightening of his larynx. Friend or no friend, you never want to tell Adolfo what he does not want to hear. For a moment, he almost spoke the truth, then at the last second he said, "Right on target, Presidente. We are in final testing. We will be ready for full-scale production within one year, just as planned."

"You mean six months," responded Adolfo with a grin and a tight squeeze on Javier's shoulder.

"Now, now, Presidente," said Javier with a slight laugh, "you did tell me I still had a year to perfect the process."

"I know, my friend, I know, but things are getting tougher. Our people could sure use a lift."

"All I can do is try, Presidente. I can promise you that I will try. Happy Birthday, Presidente" said Javier as he walked away.

The birthday dinner party was in and of itself lavish. When contrasted by the stark poverty in the streets below, it was truly gluttonous. Servants in lily-white uniforms hustled by with trays packed full of the world's finest foods. Caviar from Russia was served alongside thinly sliced Jamon Serrano from Spain. French cheeses and longostinos from Chile girdled the ice statues depicting the revolution. Basanta could only smile as he watched his loyal followers jump at his every suggestion. They knew very well what it was like to be on the outside. These dinner parties were but a simple way to keep their allegiance.

The president, having been married numerous times, had finally decided to swear off any serious relationships. With his power and prominence, being faithful was out of the question. Too many young ladies had always been waiting in line to have a taste of the power. Even at 71, for some reason the women could not stay away. Having given up cigars, one of his few remaining weaknesses was for a good-looking woman in a short skirt.

Tonight was no exception. General Ruiz had introduced him to a breathtaking young lady not more than 29 years old. Her light brown hair and green eyes framed a face as beautiful as any he had ever seen. Even as the general had introduced Maria as his date, Basanta had secretly decided he wanted this woman.

Maria Mercedes Bazan had grown up in a small village just outside of Havana. Her family had decided to stay when many of their relatives had picked up and left for Miami. Her childhood was quite normal. Her family was full of love and quite close. Unbeknownst to her, however, her father, along with several other men in her village, had decided that they had enough of Basanta. In what turned out to be a poorly planned raid, the men had been caught red-handed trying to eliminate the problem. The president had decided to make an example of the failed assassination attempt. The court was a farce, and the trial quite speedy. To no one's surprise, the court ruled for an immediate public execution of the four men involved.

Maria was able to see her beloved father for only a few brief moments before he was killed. He was bruised and badly beaten. With his bloody lips he told her, "Maria, my sweet Maria, I am so sorry that I have failed you and your mother." He coughed a deep and raspy cough. He spit up some blood and continued: "I know this looks bad, Maria, but please forget me. Please help your mother to put this behind you both. It is no use trying to fight. We cannot win." In her last words to her father she said, "I love you, Papa, you have made me very proud. I will remember you always." With that she broke down crying. She handed him a cross that she had made from a simple palm leaf. She told him to keep it with him for strength. She was crying hysterically when a guard finally removed her from the cell.

Now it was 10 years later and she was all grown up. It took months of planning, but she was finally here. Less than 50 feet away from her stood the most evil man she had ever known. She poured her hatred into a perfect smile. She had no idea what to do next. Would he even notice her, she wondered. Her beauty, however, could not be overlooked. Adolfo could not keep his eyes off her. No matter where she went, she would look, and he would be looking at her. On several occasions he would even wink at her. With the utmost control, she would just smile and tilt her head. It was a look few men could refuse.

After several more minutes, the president motioned for

his assistant Fabiano Ramirez. "Fabian, do you see that young lady over there?" asked Basanta.

"Yes, sir, she is quite breathtaking," said Fabian.

"I would like to have a drink with her, Fabian. Please speak to the general and see if he is in agreement."

"But, sir, she is with the general."

"Ask him, Fabian. I'm quite sure he will understand. Tell him it is a birthday present for the old man," answered Adolfo.

"As you wish, Presidente," said Fabian as he shuffled across the room.

General Ruiz was quite relieved that their leader finally took the bait. He had just met Maria earlier in the week, but he knew immediately that his leader would be quite pleased and taken by her. The general knew that by occasionally bringing a gift for his leader, he would be given even more freedom and power.

The general went through great lengths to make the request seem like a big deal. Smiling as he turned away, he watched Fabian escorting his date to meet the great leader. Maria's heart raced uncontrollably. She could feel her heart beat even in her temples. Tonight even a pounding headache could not keep her from her private agenda. As she approached Basanta, she gave him her very best smile and curtsied. Fabian made the introduction as the president took her hand and kissed it lightly.

As head of security, Javier Suarez watched the president's new companion with great steadfastness. She was quite beautiful, but where did she come from? Her look spells trouble, he thought. He set the ball rolling to identify her and do a quick background check.

As they talked, the president was quite taken by her smile and warm charm. With the music and the bubbly champagne, even Maria was taken in by the ambiance of the evening. "Would you care to dance, Maria?" asked the president.

"Why, of course, Presidente," she answered, acting timid and looking down.

"Please eliminate the formalities," he responded as he gently took her hand. As they slowly danced across the polished floor, she knew she had her work cut out for her. She realized that one of the few times he would be unescorted by his security people would be in the bedroom. She had not yet figured just how to get him there, but in time she would. She smiled as his hands began caressing the soft skin of her back, which was exposed by her low-cut dress.

For Maria the evening could not have gone much better. Maria's goal tonight was to at least get him to ask to see her again, but it seemed to be going much better than even she planned. The president said, "Maria, the general has left, could I give you a ride home?"

This took Maria by surprise. She was staying at a cousin's home, yet she did not want to leave any tracks. She decided she would have to play it by ear. "That would be most gracious of you, Adolfo," answered Maria.

As the Russian-built limousine approached, a slew of people surrounded the presidente. With a sudden rush, they were hurled into the back of the car. As the car lunged forward, Maria began to laugh. "What is it, my dear?" asked Basanta.

"It's just so amazing that I am here. If you would have asked what I would be doing tonight, I would have had no idea I would be going home with the most powerful man in the Caribbean."

The president smiled to himself as he read between the lines and could once again feel the power of his position - a position he would never, ever give up. "Maria, would you like to see my palace?"

"I surely would! I have only seen pictures, I am sure it is quite beautiful," answered Maria.

Javier Suarez wasted no time picking up the champagne glass Maria had drank from. He placed the glass into a plastic bag and gave it to an assistant to have her fingerprints identified. It was standard practice to fingerprint citizens for their identity card. It was only a hunch, but something just did not smell right. Even with the power of Basanta, why had such a beautiful woman acted as she did. Something did not add up, and he was going to find out why.

The driver, as he had done on so many other occasions, took the scenic route. They drove along the old beach road. With the moon dancing across the water, Maria felt beside herself, as her dream was coming true before her eyes. As they entered the palace gates, the guard on duty quickly waved them through. The security escort that was following behind the Presidente stopped at the gate and left as soon as they were safely in the compound.

Inside the palace, Maria felt as if she had entered another world. The huge hand-carved oak doors opened into a cool foyer with Italian marble floors and West Indian mahogany paneled walls. The floors were meticulously polished to a mirror shine. The smell was a mixture of lemon furniture polish and fresh-cut flowers. Beautiful arrangements of flowers were in practically every room. Servants, who attentively took their leader's jacket, immediately greeted them. "Champagne for the lady and myself," said Basanta to an older servant who was dressed in formal black and white.

Maria's shoes made a loud tapping noise, echoing off the hard marble floor as she was escorted to a sitting room overlooking the garden. The walls were adorned with only the finest in hand-painted pieces, mostly from Spain and Portugal, along with several mosaics appearing Italian.

Maria's head began to spin as she sat down on the love seat in the sitting room. The president appeared to be quite the gentleman as he personally poured the cold champagne into two glasses. "So, what do you think of my humble home, Maria?"

"It is more than I could express with words," answered Maria with a bright smile on her face. As she looked around, she was reminded why she hated this man so intensely. She realized just how easy it would be for him to forget about the world around him, living in his lap of luxury.

Because everything had happened so quickly, she was caught off guard. Her plan had been to merely introduce herself to Basanta, and yet as fate would have it she was now almost alone with him in his palace. She knew that even with his age, she could not manage to overpower him in a struggle. When she made her move, it would have to be decisive and quick. She needed to find a weapon. She scanned each room trying to find anything. In one corner of the adjoining room stood the armor from a Spanish conquistador. In the soldier's hand was a sword made of Spanish silver. Maria could not imagine wielding something so heavy. It would have to be smaller, much smaller.

She stood up and pretended to be looking out the window, while actually looking in all directions for something. Suddenly, Maria developed an evil smile as she discovered her prize. Sitting on a bookcase was a small antique dagger. It was slightly larger than her hand as she palmed the weapon and slid it in under a ruffle on her dress.

She would need to place it somewhere a bit more secure as she continued to pretend to admire the artifacts placed around the rooms for display. "Is there someplace where I could use a lady's room?" asked Maria.

"Why, of course!" In a strong macho tone he called out to a servant, "Antonio, take the lady to the guest bathroom."

"Certainly, Presidente, please follow me, señorita." As Antonio led the way, Maria walked quite uncomfortably trying to keep the dagger hidden in the loose ruffle of her dress.

As Maria was in the bathroom placing the dagger securely beneath her dress, she heard the quick chirp of tires as a car stopped quickly on the cobblestone drive outside. As she exited the room and walked into the sitting room, she saw a man in a dark suit rush into the room toward Basanta. "Are you all right, your Excellency?" asked Javier Suarez, almost out of breath.

Visibly upset about being interrupted, he said, "Yes, of course, you idiot, why shouldn't I be?"

"Your Excellency, do you know who this pretty young lady is?" asked Javier.

"She is a good friend of General Ruiz," he answered.

"Sir, in his haste to please you, the general has failed you boorishly," said Javier with a satisfied, smug look on his face. "He never ran a security check on her. If he had, General Ruiz would easily have found her dangerous past. "

Although calm on the outside, Maria's heart pounded as she tried to look innocent. Javier handed the president the report hastily torn off a computer printer, with a colored picture of Maria. The president grunted as he digested the report's meaning.

"So, Maria, what is your intention? It could not be to merely sleep with me? Did you plan to try to finish your father's work?"

"My father was an unfortunate victim of misguided friends, your Excellency. His death was a terrible tragedy, but I do not believe in his cause." As convincing as her sweet smile and innocent eyes reflected, Basanta did not buy it.

"Take her away, Javier, and thank you for your diligence," he ordered.

"As you wish, your Eminence, and what would you like me to do with her? We have no hard evidence to convict her, only her past."

"I do not care, just get her the hell out of here!" he exclaimed, waving his right hand wildly.

Javier escorted Maria into his car. They entered on his side of the vehicle and she slid across the seat. "What are you going to do with me? I demand you drop me off in town immediately!"

"I'm not sure what I am going to do with you. Give me your purse," demanded Javier. He dumped the contents in her lap as he began rummaging through the contents.

He found nothing incriminating in the purse, but looking down into her lap, he saw something awfully tempting. Her legs looked soft and supple. As he looked up at her, he could not help noticing her firm, full breasts. He decided he would not just get rid of her without at least a little reward for his hard work.

It was getting late. He was on his way to see Ernesto Gonzalez in the morning, at the Nautilus Project laboratory. He decided it would not hurt to bring the young lady with him. He would at least enjoy the companionship. "I will take you to the station tomorrow by noon. Until then we must go to Cardenas for an important meeting in the morning. You will not be harmed unless you decide to be difficult."

The ride was long and dark. No matter how humorous and jovial Javier tried to appear, Maria could not relax and she remained reticent. As she looked at the large scar on his face, fear drove her now. She only wanted to survive this night, and her chances were very slim. She tried to remain calm on the outside even as her inside churned.

CHAPTER NINETEEN

Two hours of sleep had only been a tease to Jim's body. As Larry knocked on the door, Jim's body actually hurt, as he slowly, once again became conscious. "Is it 2 already?" asked Jim, like a schoolboy not wanting to get up.

"Yeah, afraid so. Charlie's already up, and Ricardo is ready to fire up the gunboat," said Larry.

Jim sat up and slowly began getting dressed. He gathered his sea bag and headed for the Cuban vessel. He stored his belongings with the rest of his gear and headed for the bridge. Charlie was ready with some strong warm coffee for Jim.

The rich taste of the coffee felt good, as Jim quickly became alert. Jim started to get a feeling of excitement he had not experienced in many years. It took him back to the years of his childhood. For a moment he remembered the many times he had been awakened as a child and shuffled into a car to go camping. This morning the destination was quite different, but the excitement of the quiet morning was just the same. As they sat on the bridge and looked up at the stars, it felt as if they were the only people on the planet awake. In truth, with the exception of a submarine cruising just off the Cay Sal Bank, they were the only people around for many miles.

As the engines slid into gear and the throttles moved forward, Charlie turned to his brother and gave him a reassuring smile. In the pale moonlight it was difficult to see waves breaking on the reef ahead of them. Charlie had brought his hand-held GPS, Global Positioning System. When they found the safe passage in the daylight, Charlie had earlier recorded the position of the pass.

"Three-hundred-forty-two degrees and two-tenths of a mile, Ricardo," instructed Charlie. It was the first time Ricardo had seen this portable navigation device. Cuba did not use many GPS units. For many years the U.S. military scrambled the signal. This reduced the military effectiveness of the units used by other countries picking up the free satellite signal. In fact, it was Desert Storm that gave the GPS its claim to fame. Troops first used the device in the desert combat, and the units worked flawlessly.

Ricardo was amazed at just how precise this new navigational tool was. He cleared the reef line effortlessly. With a gentle, rolling sea, Ricardo plotted a course for the shipyard. In a few minutes Jim went back below to catch an extra hour of his needed sleep. As Jim lay in his bunk, it felt strange not to carry the weight of being the captain of the vessel. It was comforting to know that someone else was in charge. For the time being, Jim could just relax and leave the worrying to Captain Ricardo.

After a deep, solid nap, Jim heard the engines whine down as Ricardo backed off the throttles. He got up and made his way top side. When Jim made it up to the bridge, he found the two brothers looking intently into the distance. As Jim looked out the forward window, he saw for the first time the lights of Cuba reflected into the night sky. For being such a relatively short distance from the Keys, it seemed like another ocean away. The shapes of large mountains could be seen reflected off the lights of the city.

Three miles before them was a white flashing light. Ricardo counted in Spanish, one 1,000, two 1,000. The light flashed again. "That's our baby! That light is the mid-channel marker for the entrance to the Mantanzas River," said Ricardo. Jim understood enough Spanish and international rules of the sea to know what Ricardo was talking about.

Ricardo quickly made the proper adjustments, and they headed directly for the channel. There is always a strange feeling when you reach foreign soil by boat. Jim and Charlie felt good as they passed the lit marker and followed the unlit markers guiding them through the river mouth.

The coffee-colored water from the outflow of the river was met in direct opposition to the incoming salt-water tide. This made for quite choppy conditions at the river mouth. Jim could just picture the predatory fish lurking just below the surface, waiting for helpless prey from the river to cross their path.

The river was empty of boat traffic, and in a short time they made it to the government maintenance facility. The facility had the look of a tired shipyard and was not as large as one might have imagined. There was room for just four ships and a huge hoist used to lift a ship out of the water and onto dry dock. The rusty I-beams looked to have been put into service several decades earlier. Oxidized sheet metal littered the grounds with no apparent order.

There was only one vessel tied to the dock and a couple of others getting bottom work done in the yard. The other vessel, a 35-foot "go fast" cigarette boat, was bright red and looked sparkling new. It looked completely out of place in the dilapidated boat yard. On the boat's wind-shield, a large fluorescent green sign was affixed. In the glow given off by the dock lights they could read that the boat had for some unknown reason become the proper-ty of the Cuban people.

Looking down, Charlie wondered how the boat had been procured. Was it drugs or some spirited family from Miami coming in hopes of picking up relatives? As they tied up, Jim remained below until given the all-clear sign from Charlie. They were right on schedule. It was 4:48 a.m. and the place was as empty and eerie as a graveyard in the loneliness of night.

Ricardo went to the main building to look for the vehi-cle that is kept for officers on shore leave. It was an old 1958 Chevy in surprisingly good shape. The car was a two-tone baby blue and white. It even had white-walled tires that looked quite old. Ricardo was glad to find the large American car. It had a lot more trunk room than the Soviet alternative. As Ricardo turned the key, he was astonished to hear the old car roar to life. With the loud rumble of the motor, Ricardo pulled the car beside the docked vessel.

In a matter of seconds the gear was transferred and the car trunk closed. As planned, this day was a national hol-iday in Cuba celebrating Adolfo's birthday. The mainte-nance facility would be closed until tomorrow. By tonight they would be long gone.

CHAPTER TWENTY

Now on foreign soil, Jim felt strange as Ricardo drove the narrow streets, and they made their way into Cardenas. Looking decidedly Third World, they passed old men walking with mules pulling wooden carts loaded with cut wood and sugar cane. It was still quite early and fairly cool. Soon, even with the holiday, the town would come to life.

Entering Cardenas, they drove several times around the block where Nautilus Project was housed. The drab buildings of the town appeared old. They were in dire need of a good cleaning and several fresh coats of paint. Numerous wires were hastily tacked on the outsides of the structures. Most rooftops were missing barrel roof tiles and looked weathered and in disrepair.

Everything remained quiet as they slowly eased by the unsuspecting inhabitants. Ricardo found Ernesto Gonzalez's apartment just down the street. As they peered into the open window in his second floor apartment, they could clearly see Ernesto home.

Wearing a garnet-colored velour bathrobe, he was reading the paper and drinking his morning cafe con leche. Charlie felt pretty good as he looked around and realized that Ernesto was all alone. Snatching him would be easy pickings. The plan called for Jim to drop Ricardo and Charlie off at the project building. They were to set the plastic explosives while Jim would wait in the car for the brothers' return. In less than two hours, their mission would be complete, and they would be heading out of town.

According to intelligence reports, the laboratory would have only a skeleton crew working during the holiday. Getting in would be difficult but only a small challenge for Charlie. As planned, they ate breakfast at the small outdoor café across the street from the laboratory. It was Charlie's first meal in his homeland in many years. Charlie enjoyed sitting at the quaint café and ordering his meal in Spanish. It was not too different from any of the many restaurants on Eighth Street in Miami, also known as Calle Ocho. Three old men stood at the window and ordered coladas of Cuban coffee and flirted with the heavyset waitress. Four men with long thick cigars sat at a table, cussing as they played an early game of dominoes.

Charlie and Ricardo did not witness much activity across the street. After several quiet minutes, Charlie and Ricardo picked up their canvas bag and headed for a building next door to the laboratory.

Back at Ernesto's apartment, everything was also peaceful. Jim sat in the old car pretending to read a news-paper he had found under the driver's seat. Suddenly a car pulled up in front of the complex. An official-looking man with a scarred face got out of the car and headed for the passenger door. Jim immediately noticed a beautiful woman being escorted from the car. The man appeared to grab the woman quite firmly by the arm as he led her to the main apartment entrance.

Ernesto's building was also old. The paint was almost completely peeled from the walls facing the street. The door, made from iron bars, had many coats of chipped black paint. The elevator had long ago stopped working, so the man and woman took the stairs. Jim was cautious as he got out of the car to get a closer look. Sure enough the couple entered the second-floor apartment. In a few minutes, loud, tense voices could be heard, as the intense-looking uniformed man was demanding answers.

"You fool, how much longer can you expect to play your little games," said the intelligence director, Javier Suarez. Ernesto almost cowered in the corner as Javier berated him. "I am so very close, today I will have the answer, you have my word. Last night the final test was extremely promising," answered Ernesto timidly.

To himself he realized that this would have never happened in the West. In the West he would be treated with respect. He would be working in a state-of-the-art facility, not this old cigar factory. Still, life for him was better than for most. At least he had perks that even a doctor here did not receive.

Javier said, "We will go there at once, and you had better be right! If you do not give me some results, this entire project will be shut down!" Javier led them into the hall and down the stairs to the car below. To himself he was surprised he had spoken so openly in front of the woman. But he knew that she would not be around long. He had planned to be out of Cardenas soon. He would take her to his beach house. There he would properly interrogate her. What was left of her would be dumped on a lonely street only to end up in the Havana morgue.

Jim turned the key and started the old chevy. As Javier's car pulled away, Jim slid the shifter in gear and with a loud clank from the transmission, he began following. The ride was short, and Jim became quite anxious as they double-parked directly in front of the old cigar factory. Trying to appear inconspicuous, Jim circled the block and found a parking space with a good view of the lab just down the street.

Charlie and Ricardo slid down the narrow air shaft of the adjoining building and made it to the wall separating the two buildings on the second floor. The building plans indicated that a window had been sealed when they built the new building against the old cigar factory. It was a long shot, but they began to drill a hole in the wall where the window should have been. As fate would have it, they only encountered solid concrete.

With concern on their faces they drilled a second hole 2 feet from the first. This time they hit pay dirt. The drill hit soft, rotten wood. Enlarging the hole, they found the framework that had hastily filled the old window on the laboratory. After making the hole barely large enough for the men to crawl through, they slipped through the opening.

As planned, the opening was just out of range of the cameras. Careful to elude the numerous cameras, Charlie began to remove the explosives from his bag and secure them to the wall around the lab. With the explosives in place, Charlie spoke softly and said, "Ricky, go ahead and set the detonator for 15 minutes." Ricardo felt quite strange setting a bomb on his motherland, but he turned the dial and put it in place.

Ricardo was about to push the red detonator button when they heard a voice. "Up here, up here. The experiment is upstairs," came the nervous voice of Ernesto Gonzalez. The three made their way into the vault in the room next to Charlie and Ricardo. Ricardo put his finger to his lips to make sure Charlie did not say anything.

Donning special protective clothing and gloves, they entered the room. Ernesto flicked a switch and fluorescent lights overhead flickered momentarily, then lit up the room in a pasty yellow white.

Ernesto's eyes lit up with joy. His calculations had worked perfectly. As he drew a biologically sealed slide and put it under his microscope he witnessed the hungry bacteria still gobbling up the radioactive waste. Only the U-235 enriched uranium remained. Ernesto's confidence soured as he stepped back to let Javier Suarez witness his idea in action. Javier had no idea what he was looking at. He very well suspected that this was all a facade by a desperate man. "You had better be telling me the truth. I will call Adolfo at once. If these results are in any way falsified, you will be a dead man," said Javier.

As if to underscore the evilness of Javier, he reached in his coat pocket and removed a hypodermic syringe. Placing it in the test tube, he pulled, creating suction, and drew in the nuclear liquid. Walking up to Ernesto, he reached down and rolled up Ernesto's sleeve.

"What the hell are you doing, I'll be dead in minutes!" screamed a panicked Ernesto.

"You have been playing with me for too long, I have had enough!"

In the other room, Charlie looked at Ricardo. "What should we do?" asked Charlie with his eyes. Ricardo simply shrugged his shoulders. They decided to wait.

Placing the point of the needle against Ernesto's flesh hard enough to make an indentation in his skin, Javier looked long and hard in Ernesto's eyes. Ernesto's eyes were wide white with fear. After several tense moments, Javier put down the needle.

"Just wanted to make sure you were not bullshitting me again," said Javier coldly.

Rolling down his sleeve, Ernesto wiped his sweaty brow with his arm. "I am not bullshitting you! This is the real thing, I am telling you, I have pure plutonium here," said a shaken Ernesto.

With the plan getting worse at every turn, Charlie and

Ricardo had no idea what to do next. Do they wait for them to leave or should they intercede? Confronting them now would be the only answer. If they blow up the room now, they will take with them the project's secrets. If they wait until they leave, the secret would be out. Charlie reached for his weapon and made sure the silencer was in place. Once in the open, the cameras would quickly alarm the security personnel that something was awry.

"Wait here, brother, I must go below and silence the cameras. You wait for my return," said Charlie. Taking out innocent people was difficult even for a soldier like Charlie. Because they were also soldiers, it would be easier, but Charlie realized that this was not exactly a volunteer army. Eluding the cameras would be impossible. His survival would depend upon moving with quicksilver speed and silence. Stealth would once again be his best weapon.

The one thing working in Charlie's favor was the fact that the soldiers on duty were all too busy checking out the beautiful girl Maria. They were not expecting an intruder from above. In less than three seconds Charlie raced down the stairs and flew feet first into the duty station. As Charlie entered the room, he immediately began shooting at the communications equipment on the shelf in front of the men. He stood still for a moment, giving the men the fierce look of a warrior. Through either complacency or utter terror, the men just froze with eyes wide as saucers.

One of the men started reaching for his side arm, but then realized that doing so would be equivalent to ordering his own execution.

"Do it, and you will be dead before you hit the floor," said Charlie in a deep Spanish voice.

All at once, the four men on duty put their hands high in the air. Charlie felt lucky as he watched the last remaining video monitors and could for the first time see the beautiful girl and the scurrilous-looking officer.

Ricardo's apprehension grew with each passing second awaiting his brother's return. What had happened to him? Had he been caught? It was taking too long. Finally a shadow entered the room. "It is done, my brother, I have disarmed the guards and locked them in the office below, but I did not have time to search for additional weapons. They will not stay put long, we must work fast," said Charlie.

In one fluid movement they stormed into the vault. With their weapons pointed at Ernesto and Javier, the two registered only surprise on their faces as they instinctively put their hands in the air.

"Who are you and what do you want?" asked Javier.

"We are here for the doctor. We do not concern you. If you do not resist us, you will live and not be harmed," answered Charlie.

CHAPTER TWENTY-ONE

J im had been sitting outside the laboratory for what felt like forever. His hands were white as he gripped the steering wheel in anxious anticipation of what to do next. It took perseverance to control his urge to hop out the car and enter the building after his friends.

For Charlie it was business as usual, as he reached in his bag and grabbed some rope and tossed it to his brother. "Ricardo, I will go downstairs and tie up the guards. You take these three and start taking them out the way we came in," said Charlie.

"I do not know who you are, but you will pay for this with your life!" said Javier with staunch anger in his voice. Maria did not know what to think. She felt so out of place, just along for the ride. Just who were the good guys?, she thought.

"Shut up and follow my orders. If you make any move to resist me, I will not hesitate to splatter your brains against that wall," said Charlie with authority.

As Ricardo listened to his brother, it finally dawned on him just who this intelligence officer was. He motioned his brother to come over, then whispered his name and position in his brother's ear. "I see," said Charlie to his brother. Charlie was very well informed of the evilness of the man before him. It was common knowledge that he had even experimented on orphaned children, trying different interrogation techniques.

"Do we take him with us, or do we lock him in the vault?" asked Charlie.

"It is up to you, but a quick death would be too good for him. We should take him with us," answered the brother.

As Ricardo tried forcing the fat man through the fairly narrow opening, Charlie made his way downstairs. Ricardo pointed to the flashing timers on the C-4 detonators, encouraging the three to move quickly.

Entering the office, Charlie quickly counted the soldiers. Glancing around again, he counted only four. He suddenly remembered there was supposed to be five on duty. Oblivious to what had happened just moments before, a young soldier named Perez had been reading the morning news and relieving himself. As he left the bathroom and turned the corner, he saw the stranger holding a silenced automatic weapon on his comrades.

Through either eagerness or lack of combat experience, he immediately reached for his side arm and fired off a poor shot, shattering the plate glass office window. Fragments of glass flew everywhere. Quickly dropping to his right knee and turning, Charlie fired off three fast bursts from his silenced weapon, sounding more like muffled thuds than actual bullets. He struck Perez solidly in his chest. Charlie then turned back around to find the four remaining guards drawing weapons from a concealed weapons.

Rather than wage a battle at such short range, he leaped through the broken window and vaulted up the first half of the flight of stairs. Taking a defensive position, he raised his arm to shoot. As the first guard turned up the stairs, Charlie was ready. Although the guard did manage a burst from his weapon, it was only a reflex as he was hit in the head and falling to the floor. With the remaining three at bay, Ricardo yelled at his brother, "You OK down there?"

"I am fine, I will be behind you. Get them out first; I will hold them off and give you time."

Five minutes went by, and Charlie began a silent retreat up the remaining steps and into the laboratory. As he opened the door, a burst of automatic weapon fire ricocheted in the stairwell. Now in the lab, Charlie could clearly see the timers on the detonators. He had 2 minutes and 15 seconds left. He had thought about resetting them, but he still would need to be able to get out. He would have to wait just a little longer. If he gave the soldiers too much time up here, they would stop the explosion. If he vacillated too long, he would be part of it.

Just when he was ready to go for the opening, more shots rang up from the stairwell. Blindly firing back, he could see that they had turned the corner and were just outside. Quickly removing the silencer and loading a fresh magazine of cartridges, he fired more rounds loudly and blindly to keep them off guard.

Looking back at the timers, he saw that he now had only 12 seconds left. Hearing footsteps, he realized that it was hopeless to escape. Opening the stairwell door, he fired off more shots. He could hear screaming as these shots hit home. Then with only 4 seconds left he flew across the room and into the hole.

The explosion could be felt in every bone in Charlie's body as he was thrown down the airshaft and hit the floor below. His lungs felt as if they had collapsed from the concussion of the explosion. Dust and debris enveloped him as he hit the hard surface below. Large chunks of brick and cement fell down on him. The last thing Charlie remembered as he lost consciousness was the warm salty taste of blood in his mouth.

Waiting until the very last moment for his brother, Ricardo finally looked at his watch and yelled, "All right, let's move, start running."

With his gun drawn, the three men and the woman began running for their lives. As the building behind them exploded, Ricardo - with his eardrums nearly ruptured by the deep, dull sound of the blast - began running slower and slower as if suddenly out of fuel. For Ricardo, reality was immediate and painful. For him it meant that the mission he had so carefully planed had killed his only brother. He felt deep anger at never again being able to see him.

Sitting just down the street, Jim watched the explosion with terror on his face. He had not seen Charlie exit with the others and realized something had gone terribly wrong. Jim cranked the car and in one fluid motion put the car in gear and hit the accelerator. The wheels squealed on the damp cobblestone. He stopped in front of them and flung the car doors open. Without any words spoken four people jumped into the car.

Pausing momentarily, Jim looked toward Ricardo for direction. Sadly, Ricardo said, "We lost him, let's get the hell out of here." Jim grimaced in agony as he looked down and then hit the accelerator pedal.

The three hostages did not make a sound or put up any resistance as they quickly sped down the streets leading back to the boat yard. Usually due to familiarity, a return trip appears at least to take less time. This trip, however, seemed to take an eternity for Jim as he tightly gripped the wheel. With the windows rolled down, the warm dusty salt air swirled around the speeding vehicle. It was now 10:30; they were 25 minutes behind schedule. Ricardo was hoping the maintenance facility would still be empty of people and activity.

The blast had been extraordinary and had affected a large circumference around the site. For several blocks in all directions windows were blown out of buildings. Fire and an immense cloud of dust came out of the crumbling rubble that was once a building. Sirens were still wailing as Jim's car exited the city.

Their plan had not called for the taking of any prisoners other than Ernesto Gonzalez. In their haste to get away, however, they had no choice but to take the rest. Ricardo convinced himself he had made the right choice.

The old men playing dominoes, though shaken, were unharmed. Unfortunately for Jim, they had gotten a good look at the old Chevy. Soon after the disturbance, they began talking loudly to each other using wild hand movements. Each of the men had a differing story of what had just transpired. Before any police could broadcast a description of the Chevy over their radios, the car had sped out of town.

"Hurry! Get them on board!" ordered Ricardo.

After unloading passengers, Jim backed the car under a mango tree beside the main building. With the position of the car, it could only be seen from the river. He quickly ran across the poorly paved lot and jumped aboard the vessel. Ricardo hurried up to the wheelhouse and fired up the diesels. With a loud roar the engines came to life. Ricardo increased the throttles in order for the engines to warm up as fast as possible.

Jim also made his way up to the wheelhouse and placed a hand on Ricardo's shoulder.

"Ricardo, I know this is frickin' crazy, but I can't leave. I would never be able to live with myself if I did not at least try and free John Kelly," said Jim somberly.

"You go back, get your wife and get the hell out of here. I will stay behind like John did for me many years ago. I'll make sure you get out of the facility without being pursued."

"Jim," Ricardo said, pausing and looking Jim directly in his eyes. "We've made it. We are almost out. The laboratory has been blown up. Now we need to get the hell out of here. How do you think I feel? I planned the Cuban part of the mission and my own flesh and blood is lying back there, crushed under several hundred tons of brick and mortar. All we can do now is go forward. We cannot look back or even sideways. Let's just toss the dock lines and we are free of this stinking country. Besides, we have people still counting on us. My wife Ana and your mate are waiting for us in Cay Sal. If we go to the prison now, I can feel it in my bones, it will be trouble! Besides, what in the hell do we do with our prisoners?"

"Can't we lock them up in a cabin or something? I'm sure you've had prisoners on board before."

"Sure, but I always had one of my men watching them. We can't just lock them up in crews' sleeping quarters and just hope they stay put? Taking Ernesto Gonzalez with us is out of the question," answered Ricardo. "How in the hell do you plan on getting in and out of the prison? I've been there, we can't just walk in and simply demand your friend."

"Ricardo, right now all I have is a few ideas. I was really counting on your brother, especially his Spanish. Even on my own, however, I've got to at least give it my best shot, even if I get caught. If I left two of my closest friends and fellow soldiers behind on the same island, I could never again look at myself in a mirror."

"What was your plan before, with my brother?"

"We have several basic ideas. The best scenario involved Charlie impersonating an officer and basically walking into the damn place. I would wait outside in order to not draw attention to my gringo good looks."

Ricardo shut down the engines and, pointing to his uniform said, "I will do it for you. I am an officer, we could also take Major Suarez along just to make sure we can get inside."

"Good idea, but he doesn't look very happy. I don't think he will go along, at least not without a fight? I think it best we lock up all three prisoners and if you would go along, go in together. Could I not be a Russian intelligence officer or something?"

"Sure, hell, it might just work. I know my brother would want me to at least try." Ricardo said this without confidence, with a degree of reservation.

"Ricardo, do you have a typewriter and a fax machine on board?"

"I do," said Ricardo with a look of intrigue.

"Does your fax machine make copies?"

"Yes."

"What if you drafted a note from the powerful and once mighty Major Javier Suarez? The note would order you to escort me, to pick up John Kelly. Let's say the Russians needed to borrow him for a few days to interrogate him about United States submarine warfare tactics. What if you had him sign it and made a copy of his military identification?"

"I think you will have carte blanche access to the prison and John Kelly, my friend."

In a matter of minutes, the note was drafted, typed and signed. With the encouragement of a sharp object poking in the side of his ribs and a cloth gag wrapped tightly around his jaw, the lieutenant did not put up much of a fuss.

With the three securely locked in the crew's cabin, Ricardo and Jim got into the old Chevy. It was risky using the same vehicle, but they had no choice. Ricardo drove, as they turned out of the complex and onto the dirt and gravel road. The road was in bad condition with numerous potholes. The old Chevy had shock absorbers that were decades old. At times they felt as if they were traveling down the road on a pogo stick instead of a sedan.

Stopping just outside the penitentiary's main entrance, they pulled over to have a better look around. Using binoculars, Jim quickly counted heads of the guards on duty. Thankful for the holiday, Jim said, "Doesn't look too bad. Now just to get John out."

Ricardo drove up with purpose and confidence. The two got out of the rusty old car and walked unabashedly to the front gate.

The weathered garrison appeared to be several centuries old. The sandy brown walls looked massive and quite impregnable. The architecture was unmistakably Spanish. Entering the main archway, there was a bulky black iron door in front of them, to their left, a small office. Inside, behind a heavy wooden desk, a heavyset guard was on duty. The soldier appeared quite uncomfortable, dripping in perspiration. His oscillating fan, blowing on high, was trying to clear the room of bad body odors and the hot stagnant air. The guard never even looked up from his newspaper as he reached out and in Spanish said, "Papers, please."

Ricardo reached in his pocket and casually handed the guard his papers. With much trepidation, Jim stood and waited for an expression of some kind from the guard. At the end of the letter, the soldier's demeanor changed entirely. He appeared puzzled. Jim gently touched his side arm, hidden beneath his shirt for reassurance. The guard looked up at them with an almost blank stare.

Oh shit, he's on to us, thought Jim as he looked over to Ricardo. What if he had already heard about the bombing and the car's description over his communications radio?

Standing up, the guard smiled and said, "Welcome, gentlemen. I've never received orders directly from Major

Javier Suarez, this is quite unusual. I'm going to need authorization. Let me get the commanding officer and we will see if we can get you out of here in short order."

Pressing the intercom button, he asked for someone to come to the office and retrieve the letter. In a few seconds, a pass-through window was opened and the documents were handed to someone on the inside.

For Jim, the opening of the gate seemed to take an eternity. Christ's sake, we're loosing time, guys, let's go, we've got to get moving, thought Jim.

Ricardo said, "Can you at least start getting Sr. Kelly ready, we haven't much time."

"I would, my friend, but I have never had such a request, especially without forewarning. I will need permission, I am quite sure you understand."

"Certainly, we will just have a seat over there," said Ricardo, pointing at two old wooden chairs sitting against the wall.

After a protracted 30 minutes, the tension in Jim's body became overwhelming. He tempestuously fought back the urge to begin pacing. Outwardly, however, Jim appeared calm and relaxed as he remained seated in the hard, uncomfortable chair. The chair had names and Spanish words etched into its worn finish, reminding him of Catholic school. Slowly, electric motors began to turn. The sound of gears and clanging metal made both men turn their attention to the massive iron gates. They began to open.

Almost naively, Jim expected to see the face of his long-lost friend come through the gate. Emerging, however, was a short man in an olive drab uniform. It's not going to be that easy, thought Jim.

Walking up to Ricardo and sizing him up, the man said, "I am the prison commander, Carlos Reverte. I understand that Major Javier Suarez is asking for the temporary release of one our longest-held guests. This request is highly unusual, to say the least. We have been unable to contact the director for an explanation. I am sorry, but I feel obligated to speak to him personally regarding this matter. Do you have a way to get a hold of him?"

Collecting his thoughts, Ricardo motioned for the commander to step off to the side, so as to be out of range of Jim's hearing.

The tension that had been collecting in Jim's torso was now extrapolating to his extremities. Had he made a mistake, had his bravado once again caused him to hurt people he cared for? The cost would be great this time, as he thought of Ana and Larry awaiting their return. They had already practically made it out; it was Jim who caused them to turn back.

Now off to the side, Ricardo placed his hand on the commander's shoulder. Almost indignant he said, "Do you not know who that man is over there? He is Colonel Slaven, the senior KGB man still on the island. I am told that he is not a patient man. You have kept him waiting now for an awful long time. He is not going to be happy. What they need will only take a short time, yet it is extremely important to the Russians. I suggest you call Adolfo at once and get this man John Kelly out here expeditiously. Adolfo himself is allowing this interrogation."

The commander looked genuinely concerned. Once again looking over at Jim, he nodded slowly. Turning back to Ricardo, he said, "Just give me a few minutes. He has been here a very long time."

"I understand, we will continue to wait patiently," said Ricardo.

As time silently and slowly crept by, Jim Riley continuously rehearsed their next moves to get back to Cay Sal. Once again the doors to the prison gradually began to open. Sure hope it's you this time, Johnny boy. Just don't look too excited when you see me. Hell, you must be half-crazy by now, after all that damn time by yourself; I sure would be, thought Jim.

When the gates fully opened, both Jim and Ricardo expected to witness a frail, malnourished, beaten man who had long ago given in and up on life. What appeared before them, however, was a vital, healthy John Kelly, who looked like he could easily take on the two prison guards, as they clumsily held on to his arms.

"Who the hell wants a piece of me now?" bellowed the scrappy Irish, middle-aged, John.

As John looked around the room, he immediately locked his sights on Jim. John's eyes instantly lit up. Jim discreetly waved off any welcome look with his eyes and facial features. John understood and did not overreact.

"Too bad you guys can't keep him. This one is a pain in the ass," said the guard, chuckling. "Here are the keys, but I sure as hell would keep him restrained. We call him 'Loco' because he behaves like he has nothing to lose."

Ricardo placed a hand on John's head, protecting him from bumping into the car's roof as he was placed in the back seat. John appeared quite bewildered. He knew that he was finally getting out, but was not sure who the players were. As he sat down, he tumbled over due to the shackles restraining his hands behind his back. He could not brace himself and landed face first on the extremely hot plastic seat cover.

Jim helped from the other side, and as he leaned over him, he said softly, "See, just like we learned back in training, eventually we always do come back for our own."

John smiled slightly and said, "Sure took you long enough."

As Jim and Ricardo both got in the car, Ricardo started the car and cautiously put the car in gear.

Once outside the prison compound, Jim turned around to John. "John, this is Ricardo Balart, Charlie Balart's brother. I just found out a few days ago that you were alive. After all this time, I figured that you did not make it."

Now unshackled, John reached out and placed a hand on Jim's shoulder and said, "Thanks, Jim, I was always confident you would come back for me. Hell, I wish I'd known it would be today. I would have at least shaved."

Sitting back in his seat, he began to look around at the day before him. All at once John was overcome with emotion. It was a moment he had been looking forward to for so many years, yet the sudden rush of freedom had come so unexpectedly, without warning. Only an hour earlier he was settling in for another day of working out and keeping himself fit.

Now, although still on the island, he felt he was actually free. Placing an arm out the car window, he reached out and felt the warm tropical air rushing against the hairs on his arm and hand. After being locked up for two and a half decades, he could finally breathe fresh air again.

Jim let him be for a few minutes. He knew that a lot must be going through his mind right now. The three men continued on in silence until they were almost to the maintenance facility. Then Jim quickly filled John in on the remainder of the mission.

Once again, they parked the car and boarded the Cuban gun boat. After checking to make sure their prisoners were still secure, Ricardo went to the helm and with the clanging of a warning bell both engines roared to life. Jim and John untied the dock lines and Ricardo prepared to get under way.

Ricardo reduced the engines to idle and with the port engine in reverse and the starboard in forward he made a 180-degree turn and began making his way down river. In order to appear normal, Ricardo made no effort to speed toward to ocean. Instead, he leisurely cruised down river with a steady, deep rumble from the engines. Looking back, with every turn down the river, the town faded in the distance. With each bend in the river, they became more confident in their escape. With only one route to follow down the river, it was decided to let Jim pilot the vessel. Ricardo would keep an eye on the guests below. Although appearing fit, John was not prepared to serve any guard duty yet. Instead, John remained with Jim and they caught up on old times and the present.

Even with the company, it felt peculiar for Jim to be piloting a foreign vessel. The old boat felt heavy as she churned away down river to the sea. From the bridge Jim had a good view 360 degrees around the boat. As Jim looked back, he could see the dark diesel fumes come up from the water below and billow into the clear morning air. The wheel, though shiny stainless steel, had been worn in spots from years of Ricardo's diligent hand. Jim wondered how it had been for Ricardo. The storms, the endless boredom, the rafters and the drug smugglers; Ricardo had seen them all. Yet through it all, the one thing he wanted most was his freedom.

Below, Ricardo had the prisoners sit down at the galley. They were all quiet as they took seats around the mess table. On the bridge, Jim took a second look back. He thought he saw black engine smoke rising about a half a mile behind their vessel. Could it be another boat coming after us, he thought. He leaned out the window to try to listen for another engine, but it was no use. The diesels on this boat were much too loud.

Looking around he decided he would pull back on the throttles. Jim once again leaned out the window to have a listen. Yes indeed, another boat was approaching from behind the last bend in the river. "Do you hear that?" asked Jim to Ricardo as he entered the bridge.

"Yes, sounds like another patrol boat from the sound of her," said Ricardo.

"Go below and make everyone stay quiet and keep a low profile," Ricardo asked of Jim. Jim quickly made his way down the steps and into the hallway leading toward the galley. Ricardo fired up his radio and listened for any activity. From behind him he could clearly see the patrol boat overtaking him. Not wanting to look the least bit concerned, Ricardo held his present course and speed.

When the approaching vessel was less than 100 yards behind their boat, the VHF came to life. "El Matador, El Matador, El Matador, this is the Cuban patrol vessel Santa Cruz. Ricardo, are you on the bridge?" said Captain Julio Sanchez.

"Julio, is that you? What the hell do you think you're doing sneaking up on me like that," said Ricardo.

"I am sorry, but we are heading back to Havana. With that mother of a hurricane approaching, we were ordered to leave immediately," answered Julio. Ricardo was stunned. He looked as if someone had unexpectedly hit him across the face with a two-by-four.

In Cuba, unlike the U.S., weather reports were sketchy at best. There is no broadcast on a dedicated weather channel as in the United States. On clear nights the weather broadcast can sometimes be picked up from Key West, but otherwise one relies on station reports from homeport. It now occurred to Ricardo that in his haste to prepare and leave, he had not checked the tropical forecast.

"Yeah, we were going to stay here for repairs, but with the storm we were also ordered back to Santa Lucia," said Ricardo, improvising as he went along. "So what is the latest you have heard about the storm?"

"Oh, nothing I am sure you do not already know.

Antigua was flattened by Hurricane Diana. The only communication is via HAM radio stations. The U.S. National Hurricane Center still gives us only about a 20 percent chance of a direct hit, but Eastern Cuba and the entire Southern Bahamas bank are under a hurricane warning."

Holding the microphone in his right hand, Ricardo put his sweaty forehead on his left forearm and winced. The report could not have been worse. As his old friend Julio passed quickly to starboard, Ricardo wondered why Charlie had not told him about the storm, but he realized he could blame no one but himself. In the months of preparation and timing involved in a mission like this, it was easy to overlook the unpredictability of Mother Nature.

With one look back at where they had been, Ricardo continued out to sea.

CHAPTER TWENTY-TWO

The shrimp boat Beulah Pride had been steaming south toward the Florida Keys. At eight knots, top speed for Beulah Pride, her destination was the Dry Tortugas. As Capt. Philip Debouis read the weather report, he realized that with the limited speed of his boat he had crossed an imaginary line of safety. The storm had really picked up forward momentum. Computer projections were one thing, gut feelings another, but no one knew with certainty exactly where Hurricane Diana would make landfall.

For Captain Debouis, it was time to make a decision. Would the storm cross the Bahamas and head south around the tip of Florida, hitting the Gulf Coast, or would it slam eastern Florida and roll north up along the peninsula? It was anyone's guess. Computer projections had the upper level winds steering the storm to the north. Philip had a tough gamble ahead.

Already committed to being this close to the storm, it was time to roll the dice and decide whether to head back north or try to make it south out of the storm's path. Heading for port was out of the question. At least at sea, he would stand a chance. In a harbor, if the storm hit nearby, the Beulah Pride would be destroyed for sure. With minimal insurance he would take his chances at sea.

It was a tough call, but for captains, this type of decision became almost routine. After much thought, he decided to continue south. In the worst-case scenario, he would face the storm head on.

Hell, we rid'den them all out before on Beulah, thought Philip. After many years at sea, a captain encounters so many squalls and storms that it is not uncommon to feel invincible. Captain Debouis believed in the old girl. He felt she could handle anything Mother Nature dished out. During the winter they had faced wave after wave of cold fronts. "Just how much higher could the seas get?" thought Philip.

Sure, it would not be easy, but what was the worst that would happen? They would batten down hatches, clear all decks and ride her out. To Philip it was no big deal. He decided to keep the news of a hurricane away from the crew for now. No need to get them riled up.

Holding course and speed, Capt. Phillip Dubois continued south.

CHAPTER TWENTY-THREE

With the radio on, Ricardo could now hear the panicked voices of the locals as they scrambled to prepare for Hurricane Diana. Why had he not turned on the radio sooner, he thought. Once clear of the other vessel, Jim made his way back to the bridge.

"What was that all about?" asked Jim.

"Hell's about to break loose, and we are along for the ride. Ever been at sea in a category four hurricane?" asked Ricardo.

"No, cannot say that I have, only ridden them babies out from land," answered Jim.

Thinking about what lay ahead, Jim went below. As Jim was locking their guests in a room below, Ricardo looked out on the calm, still day through an open window. Everything he had worked for and the safety of Ana, the loss of his beloved brother, all ruined by a damn storm. Ricardo leaned out at the beautiful morning and, with a fist in the air, just screamed.

In a few minutes, John Kelly came back up on the bridge. Bringing fresh coffee, Ricardo reached for his cup and motioned for him to sit down. Ricardo began explaining in the best English he could muster what he had found out by talking with the other captain and listening to the radio. Jim nodded emotionlessly as he listened.

"Now let me get this right, in just less than 12 hours Hurricane Diana is going to blow through here. We will have winds in excess of 150 miles per hour, seas 50 feet or higher, and you want to know if we should proceeded with the mission," said John with a slightly raised voice.

"We cannot turn back up river for protection, we would be caught for sure. We may be able to sneak back into Santa Lucia, but it will be only that much harder to get out later," responded Ricardo.

Pointing his finger in the air John said, "Too bad we can't just call the U.S. Coast Guard and get us a damn helicopter to pick our asses up and get us the hell out of harm's way."

Ricardo nodded, "If only it was so easy. As Charlie explained earlier, this mission does not exist. We are on our own, my friend."

"If the storm is moving west at 12 knots, we will be cutting it close but we should be able to keep the storm behind us," said Jim.

He looked deep into Ricardo's eyes and could see the cold steel of determination. Even in this desperate situation you could easily see the joy of a man once held captive now alive with a taste of freedom. Immediately, the words to that Jimmy Buffett song came to mind, " I can't see an exit, but hell I'm going in."

After a long moment of silence, Jim said, "We've got no choice anyway, we have to go back anyway. Surely we can't leave your wife and my first mate on that God-forsaken rock of an island."

As they passed the last sea buoy and entered the open sea, it was a beautiful day. The sea was running 2 feet at most. In an effort to make time, they plotted a direct course for Cay Sal and proceeded on a northerly heading.

With the constant clutter of storm panic on the radio, they could not have picked a better time to leave Cuban waters.

As the men settled down and each mentally prepared for the journey that laid ahead, Jim went below to check on the prisoners. He could sense that the lady wanted no part of Ernesto or the intelligence officer. His first instinct was to interview the girl and just ask her who she was. After thinking it over, he decided it was the scientist Ernesto who he would take in the next room for questioning. He had to find out at the very least what role the girl played.

As Jim pointed the automatic weapon at Ernesto, his sweaty face revealed Ernesto's fear as he rose and quickly moved in the direction Jim pointed. "Please do not harm me," said Ernesto to his captor in a broken but understandable English.

"Have no fear, just take your first left," said Jim. Once out of the room, Jim quickly secured the lock on the galley door.

As Jim bolted the door, Javier wasted no time examining just how securely he was locked in his tiny prison cell.

As directed, Ernesto entered the room on his left. Closing the door behind them, Jim turned on a cabin light and motioned for Ernesto to take a seat. As Jim moved a chair in front of Ernesto and sat straddling the chair backward, Jim reached and grabbed the hand of Ernesto.

Jim said, "Ernesto Gonzalez, welcome to freedom. As you will learn, in the USA we treat our scientists with great respect."

With his left hand he reached under the table and brought out a bottle of coconut rum. So much for the bright white light and the cigarette burns, Jim thought. He would get the truth out of him with friendship. Ernesto had never been this scared. Looking at him, Jim could see the fear oozing from his pores. Ernesto had wanted to be important, but this was not what he had bargained for. Ernesto looked at the shot of rum before him and reached for it. He raised the clear glass and took a swallow of the warm clear liquid. He immediately felt the burn as it traveled down his throat and into his belly.

Moments later, Ernesto's face, which had been as pale as a sheet of paper, slowly began to regain a pinkish color.

Jim reached into his pocket and retrieved a large green cigar, lit it, leaned back, and in a less than an hour had the entire story told to him. Ernesto, now feeling no pain, raised his glass and cheerfully told his new friend Jim just how he had outsmarted the fascist regime in Cuba by not writing anything of consequence down. Jim tried hard to make notes, but Ernesto was speaking scientific lingo and with the broken Spanglish he was hard to follow.

Listening to Ernesto, Jim was just as happy to hear that Maria was not part of the problem as he was to hear that Ernesto had found out how to produce pure plutonium from nuclear waste. He knew he could waste no more time getting Maria away from Javier Suarez. He knew she would be feeling quite uncomfortable with him by herself. Finding out how sinister Javier Suarez was, he knew she would be in great danger.

Instead of freeing Maria immediately he had to listen to the overweight, sweaty physicist before him. He had never considered himself homophobic, but there was something about Ernesto that repelled Jim like a mosquito from a can of Deep Woods Off. Listening and taking notes, he listened for another half an hour, then stood. "Ernesto, it is clear to me that you appreciate your freedom. As a token sign of our mutual trust and respect for you, you are free to move about the ship as you please," said Jim.

Ernesto rose up and smiled. He wiped the sweat from his bloated face with a handkerchief and said, "Thank you, comrade, I will not let you down."

Javier Suarez was beside himself with anger. Never had he been in such a situation. Always the aggressor, he had never been held captive. Feeling confined, the walls, like his future, began to quickly close in on him. Trying to regain some control of the situation, he turned his anger to the women. Maria was sitting solemnly in the corner.

"It is all your fault, you bitch, you are why I am here tonight. If not for your crazy plan, I would never have been caught in this net," said Javier in a cold, bitter tone.

With a scornful look, Maria looked up and said, "Me? It was your evil intentions that put you here. I hope you rot in an American jail."

The hot Latin temper of Javier needed something to lash out at. This was just what he needed to explode. He rose up and grabbed Maria by her arm, forcing her to her feet. With the back of his right hand he slapped Maria across her right cheek, forcing her to the ground.

Through years of skilled practice, he knew the one thing he could do to make Maria truly lose her sense of self-respect and allow him to dominate her. As he had done so many times in the past few years with women he had interrogated, he decided to rape her. Reaching down, he grabbed her dress by the cleavage and pulled violently, tearing the buttons and exposing her bra. This forced Maria to fall to her right on the cold steel floor. Rolling over, she pulled up her dress, reached down and found the dagger she had tucked away.

Jim was on his way to release Maria when he heard the scream. Hurrying, he flew down the hall and unlocked the door. Jim was shocked to find Maria standing over the intelligence officer with a dagger in her hand. A fresh scar was emblazoned on Major Javier's face.

"The bastard tried to touch me!" said a hysterical Maria.

Pointing a pistol at Javier, Jim said, "Maria, you can back away and let the bad boy go. Welcome to freedom. You are free to move about as you please. Make yourself at home." Maria smiled as the tension of the past few minutes quickly relaxed off her face. Jim took her arm and guided her to the main cabin.

As they reached the deck, wind and salt spray was everywhere as the boat was running full throttle over the open sea. They climbed the steps and entered the helm area. With the exception of Javier Suarez, everyone on board was gathered there. As Jim looked at the faces of soon-to-be Cuban expatriates, he could not help but notice the gleam of satisfaction in their eyes. Even with the fear of death, with a hurricane bearing down, they all could not help but smile in satisfaction.

Ricardo watched Jim's face as he stared at the Cubans in disbelief. With one hand on the wheel, Ricardo smiled at Jim and he said, "For too long, we have been held prisoners of our dreams. Today we have been released from prison, and my friend, we have dreams no amount of wind can slow down."

"I only wish I could share this moment with my brother. He has paid the ultimate price for our freedom."

Jim nodded, listening compassionately. For the first time in his life, he understood what it meant to really be born American. He recognized just how much Americans take for granted. For the now ex-POW John Kelly, who lost the best years of his life to prison bars, freedom was just beginning to sink in.

Jim, although concerned, felt proud that they had made it this far. He realized that all he had fought for did stand for something. Never again could he look at an immigrant and not empathize with his or her situation.

CHAPTER TWENTY-FOUR

It was 2 p.m. and the sun was still high above the Mystic Lady. Overhead, a large frigate bird could be seen circling above the tiny cove. Larry and Ana had been waiting for the overdue Cuban vessel for what now seemed like an eternity. Due to the language barrier, the pair had a difficult time trying to communicate. With each passing minute they were becoming more anxious. Still they managed to remain calm and spoke with a mixture of exaggerated expressions and hand signals.

Looking up, Larry pointed out the prehistoric-looking frigate bird casting a shadow in the shallow clear water of the cove. "It is good luck," said Larry.

Ana smiled, not fully understanding him yet nodding her head. Earlier Ana had tried to remain in the cabin and out of the direct sun. The generator had been turned off to save fuel, but with the stifling heat, the cabin soon became an oven.

In the morning Larry had gone through their usual morning check list, making sure the Mystic Lady would be ready for the ride home. He had found a small leak in the hydraulic steering and was glad he had remembered to bring both extra hydraulic fluid and Teflon tape. With the repairs made, all he could do was wait.

The day had a surreal calm to it. Both he and Ana now sat on the fly bridge looking several times a minute for the Cuban vessel's return. As the afternoon sun began its slow retreat westward, it soon felt as if there was no respite from the grueling sun. Without even the slightest breeze, sweat poured from Larry's pores and streamed down his face.

Sitting at the helm, he had tried several times to listen to the radio. Yet it was to no avail; all he could pick up from this deserted spit of land was static. He had thought about trying to raise Jim on the VHV, but decided it was too risky. Larry and Ana could only wait it out.

After another 30 minutes had passed, they could not bear the heat any longer. Larry pointed to the water and pretended to swim. Ana half-smiled and nodded with a sigh. All of a sudden a refreshing cooling breeze drifted across the lagoon and over the boat.

Turning her face to the wind, Ana raised her hands in the breeze and to herself thanked the heavens. Larry removed his shirt and let the breeze evaporate his perspiration and cool his overheated body. Instead of becoming still, Larry noticed the wind actually increase slightly over the next few minutes. To himself, Larry both expected and looked forward to a cooling, refreshing typical afternoon thunderstorm.

As Larry waited for the summer squall, he began to see a steady buildup of clouds approaching from the East/Southeast. This being the predominant wind direction of the Trade Winds this time of year, Larry thought nothing of it.

With a light chop on the water over the reef, it became increasingly more difficult to make out a vessel in the distance. Straining his eyes, looking through the binoculars,

Larry thought he saw something approaching. Lowering the glass, he put his sunglasses back on and squinted as he tried to make out the object in the distance. Unable to distinguish what he thought he had seen from the white caps on the water, he waited a few moments before looking through the binoculars again. This time, however, he could distinctly make out a vessel approaching.

The ship looked to be in quite a hurry. White foam and spray masked the identity of the vessel. The smile on his face soon turned to fear, not knowing exactly what was coming toward them at such a high speed. He licked his lips nervously and could taste the salt from the dried sweat. He could sense his pulse quickening. If it was Jim, they should be traveling at a more comfortable cruising speed as to not draw attention to them.

Ana picked up on Larry's apprehension. Wiping the sweat from the lenses, he handed her the binoculars. In a matter of seconds a smile broke on her face, as she peered through the glass. "Ricardo," she said in a confident, joyful tone as she began to jump up and down with Latin emotion. Over the years she had become quite familiar with the shape of the old gunboat.

In several more minutes, the dull roar of the diesels could be heard. In another five minutes, the ship cleared the reef and made it into the harbor. As soon as the vessels were in range of each other's voices, Ricardo screamed to his wife. "Rapido, Ana, hurricane, grande hurricane!"

Larry's eyes quickly looked toward the east. Looking at the cloud formations and looking at Ricardo, he would need no interpretations. Larry cranked the engines and prepared the vessel to get under way. Jim helped secure the boats together, and in a matter of minutes passengers, supplies and a prisoner were transported to the Mystic Lady.

Larry had immediately picked up on the somber look of both Jim and Ricardo. "Where the hell is Charlie hiding?" asked Larry.

Jim looked up with a solemn face and shook his head no. "He didn't make it, Lare," said Jim. With the current situation, Larry decided not to probe any further. Until the present danger had been addressed, his curiosity would have to wait.

Before departing, Jim and Ricardo had decided to transfer fuel from the Cuban boat to the Mystic Lady. "You never know," said Jim. "With this storm approaching, it will be important to have as much fuel as heavenly possible."

Ricardo had some electric fuel pumps and the transfer was made rather quickly.

The next phase of the mission would be tough on Ricardo. Larry and Ricardo remained on El Matador while everyone else was already safely on board the sportfisherman, following the smaller boat. Ricardo could feel his belly tighten, as it became more difficult to get a full breath. As he made it out of the harbor and crossed the reef, he felt like one of his best friends was slowly dying and taking its last breath. It would be Ricardo's final act, separating his Old World and his new life in the United States. They would have to sink El Matador.

Once across the reef, they passed a series of ledges. Suddenly, the bottom began to fall away and the water became cobalt blue and deepened. As the depth sounder hit 400 feet, it was time to sink her. Like a child not wanting to go to bed at night, it was hard for Ricardo to start the sinking of El Matador. It was totally out of character for a captain to scuttle a perfectly good ship.

He stood on the bridge with his hand on the wheel. It was Larry who after several minutes said, "Ricardo, the storm's coming, got to let go, buddy."

After so many years aboard the old girl, how could he abandon her to the approaching storm? With much trepidation he realized it was time to say goodbye. Taking a crescent wrench, he backed the chrome nut holding the steering wheel in place, keeping it loosely attached, just in case they needed sudden steerage. Then he went below with Larry.

"It's hard saying goodbye, when the time really comes, isn't it?" asked Larry.

"Yes, you can plan and plan, but when the time comes to pull the life out of her, you just want one more cruise. Like one last cigarette." Pausing and looking down, Ricardo said, " I'm sorry, but she is a part of me."

Larry nodded sympathetically, then grabbed the bag of explosives and motioned for Ricardo that it was time to get on with it. As they entered the engine room, Larry carefully pressed the plastic explosives in place. Placing them in strategic locations where air and fuel would give them optimum combustible effect, they set timers for five minutes.

With the plastic in place, it was time to open the hull to the oceans and set her ablaze. "Everything is ready, let's open her sea cocks," said Larry as he opened the water intake valves below the water line. Immediately, seawater gushed in from under the hull.

Now in the bilge, Larry reached down with wire cutters and snipped the red wire powering the bilge pumps. Once disabled, nothing could now stop the huge steel ship from taking on water and going down in the building sea.

With the charges set, it was time to leave. Ricardo could feel the end of his "baby" quickly approaching. He said a quick prayer as Jim positioned the Mystic Lady alongside and they got ready to jump from the hobbled Cuban vessel. El Matador began to list slightly as she was already rapidly taking on water.

"Two minutes left, Ricardo, we've got to get out of here," said Larry.

Firmly grasping the old worn steering wheel, he removed it, then the two men jumped the final 3 feet to the Mystic Lady. Jim hit the throttles to get the Mystic Lady to a safe distance for the fireworks.

Larry had never seen, much less used, a Stinger Missile. Ricardo helped Larry set it up and load it. Placing the stinger on his shoulder, Larry motioned for Ricardo to come over. "Here, Ricardo, pull the trigger; it's your ship," said Larry.

"No, you go ahead and do it, as much as I hate what she stands for, I still cannot kill her," said Ricardo.

The first in a series of timed explosions began going off. The missile would not be needed, but it would guarantee the Cuban vessel would go down quickly. Larry wasted no more time, as he pointed the weapon and clicked the trigger. An instant after the solid click from the trigger, a white smoke trail followed the missile, and it hit home in the center of the hull.

The explosion was tremendous. Heat could be felt on their faces as the missile set off a fireball in the center of the ship. Ana covered her ears in the sudden eruption. In a fiery display, the old gray ship took on a ghastly appearance taking on even more water. In no time, the bow ceremoniously rose up into the air and, with one last moan, she slid silently into the silence of the deep blue below.

CHAPTER TWENTY-FIVE

With the winds quickly picking up, both Jim and Ricardo realized that it was time to race the storm across the Gulf Stream. They had no time to eulogize the passing of the old Cuban vessel, it was time to move on. Like any good fisherman, Jim could not resist pushing the instant save button on his GPS unit. He never knew when he would be back this way again. Jim imagined the sea life that would soon take up residence on that old Cuban gunboat.

Both captains agreed that the quickest route would be to try to make it to the Upper Keys. They would then check the direction of the storm and determine whether or not to proceed to the mainland.

Larry was stowing the mooring ropes on the Mystic Lady when he began to hear the distinct high pitch whine of outboard engines. For a moment his mind almost blocked out the all-too-familiar sound. Soon he remembered his present isolated location and looked up. In all the time he had been waiting for the others, no other boat was heard or seen; the sound was unmistakably getting louder.

Jim looked down at Larry and without words they both

began to look out at the sea. Something was coming, but they could barely make out what it was, it was approaching so quickly. The whine of the engines began to sputter as the sound got even louder. "What ever she is, she is running out of fuel. Even this old tub can outrun her. Let's get going," said Jim to Larry.

In the distance, heading directly for them, a red speed boat could be seen ripping across the water. The engines sounded like they were about to quit several times as the large motors began starving for fuel. John quickly reached for a machine gun and headed toward the bow. Jim was prepared to hit full throttle and get going in a hurry. Jim, for the first time, could see a single man on the approaching boat waving his hands wildly.

As he lowered his binoculars, Jim said, "Sure as hell looks like Charlie. It can't be!"

Everyone on the boat held their breath as they waited for confirmation of Charlie's return. Realizing it was in fact Charlie, everyone on board let out a scream. Completely out of fuel, the speedboat shut down and stopped dead in the water a hundred feet from the Mystic Lady.

Jim turned the wheel and went over to pick up his dear friend.

"Never seems to be a gas station around when you need one," said Charlie with a smug look on his bruised and battered face. Crusty dried areas of blood were glued to his cheeks.

"Thanks for that blast, I would have never found you guys without that fireball."

"My brother, you are alive!" said Ricardo as he leaped to the boat. Embracing his brother he said, "I thought we lost you back there. How did you survive the blast?"

"Last thing I remember I ended up in the bottom of a shaft. My watch broke, so I don't know how much time elapsed. I woke up to the sounds of sirens all around. I waited a few minutes in order to regain composure, then I left the building being careful to avoid being seen. I looked for you guys and realized I had most likely been out for about an hour or so. Local police were everywhere, so it was difficult to get out of the building. I was able to find a motor scooter. I got it started, and I headed for the boatyard.

"It was slow going, and my head was pounding. So by the time I made it to the yard, you all were history. Thank goodness for the cigarette boat that had been confiscated. A guard was on duty when I got there, so I had to sneak in and hot-wire her," said Charlie.

As Charlie said this, he looked toward John Kelly leaning against the railing. Charlie had either forgotten or had figured that they would naturally have aborted John's rescue. Looking dumbfounded, Charlie's face went pale, then lit up with joy, "Holy shit, John, you joined our little party!"

Charlie embraced John for a long time, then looking at Jim said, "I've died and gone to heaven." Charlie knew, as did Jim, that many sleepless nights spent in restless nightmares were over. Regardless of what they now faced, they suddenly felt whole again. Closure to an event that happened so long ago was now complete. The three Seals stood motionless reveling in the moment.

"Did you hear about our little weather problem?" asked Jim, interrupting the festive reunion.

"No, but it sure was getting choppy. Storm's coming through?" asked Charlie.

"A Cat Five blow is moving in," said Larry.

"We need to get moving if we're going to beat her," said Jim.

The wind was picking up quickly as they hit the Straits of Florida. The seas had quickly built to a solid 4 feet. To the old Bertram, 4-foot seas only allowed her to stay on plane better and actually increase her speed slightly. Back in the cockpit, Charlie looked up at the captain on the bridge. In all his years, Jim had never looked so intense. Charlie could clearly see the hidden fear in his eyes. Jim knew what lay on his plate before him. He wondered silently just what their chances were of actually making it back home.

In a half-hour a frenetic moving squall line moved through. With each moment, the seas continued to build. Cold air from high in the atmosphere blasted down in fast-moving down drafts in the minutes preceding the rain. On the bridge, Larry and Jim briefly smiled nervously, enjoying the cooling effect of the cold air.

It was 3 in the afternoon when the lightning started and rain came down in sheets. Because of the darkness of the clouds enveloping them, the day looked much later. Larry had just finished lowering the last clear Izan glass protecting the fly bridge when the rain hit like a freight train. "Must have picked up to 40-knot winds," yelled Jim to Larry.

Larry just held on as the seas quickly became 10 feet and better. "This is just the beginning. Do you think she has it in her to hold together?"

Jim answered, "Sure she will, just another windy February sailfish day, just with a little rain, my friend. Relax, just keep that EPIRB tucked under your arm" said Jim with a slight smile.

Jim had never skimped when it came to safety. On board, in addition to all the standard safety equipment one would find on a passenger vessel at sea, Jim had backup systems to almost every safety item. Jim carried three 406 MHZ EPIRBs, (emergency position indicating radio beacons). When activated, these bright orange, buoyant boxes transmit a distress signal, complete with the vessel's information, directly to an orbiting satellite.

This information is then relayed to NOAA in Washington, which in turn notifies the nearest U.S. Coast Guard search and rescue team. In this part of the world, hurricane notwithstanding, a helicopter should be overhead in 15 minutes.

The EPIRB on the fly bridge was self-deploying. In the event of a sinking, it would begin transmitting almost immediately and eject itself from the boat. Ever since installing the unit on the bridge, Jim had felt much more secure. Whether real or imagined, in tough times, like an emergency exit, it had made him feel better.

In the heavy following seas, the Mystic Lady seemed to groan as each swell would raise her transom high in the air and then slam her down as the wave moved forward with force. Even the engines would shudder as the engine's RPMs would momentarily red-line when from time to time the props would start to come out of the water.

With the deteriorating sea conditions, even Admiral Franklin could no longer risk the lives of the men on the submarine USS Baltimore. At least Charlie was on his way home and had made it out of Cuba safely. The Admiral reluctantly gave the call for the sub to head north. It was probably good that Jim did not know someone had been tracking them from below. He would have felt totally abandoned had he known that the sub was now leaving them to fend for themselves.

The admiral was able to contact the president's chief of staff, Ken Smith, and have the satellite global positioning transmitter signal unscrambled for 24 hours. For many years it used to be scrambled, to be accurate to within only 200 yards. It was the admiral's feeling that if they did reach the Keys, they would most likely be totally blind. He figured that it could only increase their chances, by making the signal accurate to within 3 meters.

Never before in all his years at sea had Jim looked at the orange box and thought he may soon need her. He opened the cover, pushed a large red button, and felt reassured when the self-test came back positive. To himself he chuckled, "What would he have done about it if the battery were low?" Still, it made him feel better knowing the EPIRB was ready if need be.

Below deck, Maria and Charlie had been talking for some time. They had gone below earlier and Maria had volunteered to help Charlie wipe the now-crusty dried blood from his face and matted hair. Ricardo tried to stay out of Jim's way and was trying hard to make his wife Ana feel comfortable in the tossing sea. Ricardo had noticed how Charlie and Maria had taken to each other. With smiles and eye movements, neither of them had any idea that outside the sea was fast becoming a hellacious world of foam and spray. They found they had a lot in common. Charlie was very impressed with the confident way she carried herself.

Unable to take the pounding, Ana was quickly becoming violently ill. Having never been seasick before, she did not know what had come over her. To herself, she thought she was going to die. Unable to take it anymore, Ricardo helped her to the head where she began vomiting the moment her face was over the bowl.

Ricardo did his best to comfort her, gently rubbing her back and telling her, "You'll feel better now."

In fact, she did begin to feel better. With an empty stomach, she began to think that it had only been something she had eaten. "You were right, I will live," said Ana in a soft, dry tone.

Ricardo smiled and kissed his wife gently on the cheek. "You get cleaned up, I need to go on top and see how Jim is doing. You will be fine."

Maria and Charlie had broken from their intense conversation when they heard Ana getting sick in the head. "We will take care of her, Ricardo, go ahead," said Charlie.

Ricardo opened the cabin door and ventured outside into the cockpit. He could not believe how angry the sea had become. With no fear in his eyes, he carefully climbed the ladder up to the fly bridge. It was difficult to hang on with the violent, jerking seas, now running a good 20 feet.

Ricardo would never forget the look of his new friends as he greeted them on the bridge. Jim looked pasty gray as he held the wheel and with each swell tried to keep the boat from broaching.

Ricardo reached in his pocket and took out a cigar. Lighting it, he handed it to Jim and said, "Been a while since you have had a true Cohiba from Havana." It was just what Jim needed to keep him from becoming too tense.

Relaxing, Jim said, "Thank you, my friend. Have you ever been in seas this tough?"

He wanted to give Jim confidence and lie, but he could not be untruthful, especially now. Putting a hand on the wheel, he said, "No, as a matter of fact, I have not, but there is always a first. Let me give you a break for a few minutes."

Jim obliged as he gave Ricardo the wheel. "It's not the height that will get you, it is how damn close these waves are together." Looking back they could see the wind actually shearing the tops off each wave as they crested. Jim could feel the tension begin to release from his shoulders as he gave Ricardo control.

Even with someone else at the wheel with the knowledge and experience of Ricardo, a captain could never truly relax. As much as he wanted to go below and get some coffee, and take a break from the blur of the sea, he remained glued to his friend's side. Only he fully knew the boat. To him, the feel of the wheel had become an extension of himself.

"What do you think of how she handles?" Jim asked Ricardo.

"For these sea conditions, she handles like a dream; for fiberglass, she sure feels heavy," said Ricardo.

As Jim looked around, he relaxed more and began to grow more confident. For the first time in the past hour or so, he actually thought that they would make it.

As he exhaled a long, slow billow of cigar smoke, he actually smiled and said, "Ricardo, this is what draws guys like us out here. It's a test of our spirit. As nice as it is on a calm day, it feels all the more successful when we make it back after a night of hell like tonight. Our spirit may be tested, but in our survival we will be better, stronger men." In Jim's eyes, he never looked more alive. With a hawk-like stare, Jim looked at his instruments and calculated his position.

CHAPTER TWENTY-SIX

Three hours and 45 minutes into the trip, they were barely making way. Visibility in the sea around them was perhaps 50 yards at best. Driving rain and howling winds now began tearing away the clear plastic Izan glass protecting the fly bridge.

"We have another station below, but I think we should stay up here. The wind already blew off my radar antenna, so we're as blind as a bat. If a freighter is around, I want as much warning as possible," said Jim to Ricardo.

All at once a loud, obnoxious alarm began buzzing. "Now what!" said Jim. As he quickly scanned his instruments, he realized the port engine was overheated.

"Must have lost another impeller blade. I'll have to shut her down," said Jim.

It was almost painful for Jim to turn the key and shut down the port engine. Jim wondered if it would ever fire up again.

He would try and restart it in a while, but for now it would need to cool down otherwise it could seize. That's why they make twin screws, he told himself. If they lost power completely, they would be done for sure. With one down, it was uncomfortable knowing they had no back-up.

What really concerned Jim was that several times in the past hour he had had to use the engines to actually steer the boat. A really large wave had lifted the transom and caused her to yaw badly; only by popping one engine in full reverse had he kept control of the boat. With that mechanism out of commission, his arsenal of defenses was greatly reduced.

In Caribbean waters for hundreds of years, there have been stories about a treacherous sea condition known by sailors only as a "White Squall." In this meteorological event, the wind would blow so hard that you had no visibility. It is similar to a whiteout during a snowstorm. With the extreme wind speed, no ship's ballast, no matter how heavy, could hold her from turning on her side and going down.

Only handfuls of sailors would survive the shipwreck and live to tell about the vicious summer winds that turned a once calm ocean into a blur of white foam. Jim began to empathize with those early sailors trying to decide if he, too, would live to talk about his adventure from hell. For once in his life he was glad to actually live in the crazy 21st Century. At least here he had EPIRBs, a life raft and a radio.

A radio, he thought. He was close enough to the Keys and yet far enough from Cuba. Besides, no one would be fool enough to pursue him in this. He thought about this a minute and then decided to grab his microphone. He made sure his radio was on channel 16.

With one more look at the dismal, deteriorating sea conditions, he keyed the microphone and said, "Securite, Securite, Securite, this is the Mystic Lady, please be advised that we are returning from the Bahamas and are located at Latitude 24.31.25 North and 080.40.59 West. We are in seas approximately 35 feet and have lost power in one engine. Our course is 333 degrees, and our speed is six knots. We are trying to beat the storm and make it to Islamorada." As Jim released the microphone, a deep raspy voice boomed back over the radio.

"Mystic Lady, this is Coast Guard Station Islamorada. Please switch and answer on channel two two alpha."

Jim turned the dial to channel 22A, a channel reserved only for Coast Guard communication, and responded. "Coast Guard Station Islamorada this is the Mystic Lady, do you copy?"

"Jim, is that you, you crazy bastard, this is Henry. What the hell are you doing out there?" answered the Coast Guard station chief. Henry was a short bald man, 46 years old. He had a red and blotchy nose that was much too large for his sun-damaged face. Henry had a heart of gold, though, and the local Conchs all loved him. Even with Jim's world crashing down around him, it helped to hear his old friend's steady voice.

"I'll explain later, my friend. I just wanted you to know I am out here," answered Jim.

"Glad you called in. We will get you home, don't you worry. I am tracking 11 other vessels in your general location. With the exception of a shrimp boat and one tug pulling a long tow barge, no one else is less than 200 feet."

"Is that supposed to make me feel better, Henry? If so, it's not working," said Jim sarcastically.

"Well, if it helps, you are the only one brave enough to issue only a Securite. Everyone else is either Pan Pan or a full-blown May Day."

In an emergency situation, there are three levels of emergency distress. The most serious of course, being a "May Day." When a "May Day" is issued, human life is in imminent danger. Usually the boat is about to go down, or there is a draconian medical emergency. Next comes the "Pan Pan" distress. A "Pan Pan" is issued when the safety of the vessel or a person is in jeopardy, but the danger is not life-threatening. A "Securite," pronounced (Saycuritay), is used to inform others about navigation problems or weather.

Jim had thought about which distress to send, but decided on the lowest level. In is own mind he did not want to admit that he was in trouble. He had to believe in his abilities. He still had a chance. His reason for the distress was twofold. First, he wanted to make sure freighters in the area knew he was there. He also wanted someone to have his position, just in case.

He had tried not to think about Linda the past few hours. He felt he had betrayed her by not telling her the whole truth. She had to be out of her mind with worry. If they had any hope of working things out, this was not going to make things any easier.

"Jimbo, seems you must have some popular guest on your boat. We have had two people calling nonstop looking for you. The first is a slightly hysterical young lady we both know only too well, named Linda. She has refused to evacuate with the rest of the Keys and is determined to wait it out at your house. The second is some admiral named George Franklin. He keeps calling as well. Do you want me to relay any messages?" asked Henry.

"Henry, tell them we are doing fine, but please ask Linda to get the hell out of there and get up to Miami. Whatever you do, don't tell Linda about the engine. If you would, however, please give the admiral our position," asked Jim.

"Will do, Jim, I better be going. We are operating with only Skally and me. Everyone else has bailed. I'll be by the radio, though. I won't leave you. Please check in every 15 minutes," said Henry.

Jim repeated his position again and signed off, "This is the Mystic Lady switching back and standing by on one six."

The winds had intensified somewhat during the conversation, yet it amazed Jim how much calmer he felt. "At least somebody knows where to start looking," Jim said jokingly to both Larry and Ricardo.

"Let me take the wheel for a while. Here is some coffee, you relax," said Ricardo.

Reluctantly, Jim let go and grabbed the cup of coffee that somehow Charlie and Maria had been able to make down below. Looking at his chart plotter and pointing to its image, Jim let out a cheer, "Look guys, we are almost home." Being blown and carried by the Gulf Stream current, even with almost no noticeable headway, they were making steady progress. "We are only 22 out, and our actual speed has increased to trolling speed, almost eight knots," said Jim.

"Should I throw out some baits, Captain?" asked Larry in jest.

The chart plotter was an onboard computer with a video screen with a cartridge containing detailed map and navigational information. The plotter zoomed into the best current location and displayed a flashing "X" where it is in relation to the map. The map gets the boat's position directly from the "Global Positioning System" wired to it. Of all the electronics on board, with the exception of the radio, the chart plotter was Jim's favorite. As the distance to go slowly decreased in increments of tenths of a mile, everyone on the bridge became more optimistic.

CHAPTER TWENTY-SEVEN

Below deck was not a pretty sight. With the exception of John, Maria and Charlie, everyone had been vomiting almost constantly in the unstable shifting world of the cabin. They had all taken seasickness pills as soon as things got rough. Unfortunately, they were taken too late. In order to really work, the pills should have been taken several hours before even leaving the docks. The worst was Ernesto Gonzalez. His face looked sunken, and his coloring was that of an avocado. As Ernesto looked down into the bucket beneath him, he seriously pondered how he could end his life.

Ana was trying to remain as still as possible amongst the violent motion of the boat. She was lying on her back in the main salon. She had taken her shoes off. For some reason she thought it would make her feel better. Maria had a moist towel and was gently wiping Ana's face and forehead.

Major Javier Suarez just wanted to be by himself. Feeling that he was the biggest security threat, Charlie insisted that he remain in the main cabin. Suarez preferred not talking with the others and would simply moan and groan as he emptied his stomach into a waste basket.

To make matters worse, the air conditioner had quit working for almost an hour. Larry had come down to try to fix it, but with the bone-jarring pounding they were taking, a hose had come loose and leaked the Freon. Without Freon in the system, it could not be repaired at sea. It was becoming totally unbearable in the cabin with no ventilation, the sweltering heat, and the sour stench of stomach contents.

Ernesto had wanted badly to run out the cabin door and throw himself on the deck. He would have given anything for the fresh air that did not wreak of vomit. He tried opening a hatch behind him, but the window may as well have been on the bottom of the hull. Water gushed in through the small opening. Charlie had to act quickly to reseal the hatch.

Charlie was not yet sick. The smell of the cabin and the motion was not exactly agreeing with him, however. "I cannot believe how frustrated and useless I feel down here," said Charlie quietly to Maria.

"Trust me, we need you here. Leave the driving to the others. I cannot handle this mess by myself," answered Maria.

"This is just not what I had planned. Nowhere had I anticipated running into a damn hurricane," said Charlie with frustration on his face.

Maria looked up at Charlie. Even in these conditions, he still looked irresistible. He was tall and strong, and Maria could tell that he was a man of deep emotion. She had only known him for such a short time, but they both could sense the chemistry between them. Maria took his hand, and placed it with hers beside her right cheek. Tears formed in her eyes as she looked at him and said,

"Charlie, believe me, this is not what I had planned, either. Yesterday, you could not have forced me to get on a boat and head for the United States. Leaving had never been an option. Today, however, it all feels right. In fact, no matter how bad it seems, there is nowhere else I would rather be right now."

Charlie could feel the power of the attraction. To himself he thought it might be the stress they were both under. She was truly beautiful. If only the circumstances had been different between them, maybe something would have developed.

In spite of being severely dehydrated, Ana had to go to the head. If nothing else, she had hoped to splash water on her face and at least cool herself. Maria assisted her, and they made their way down the hall. Stepping down the walkway to the next level, Maria immediately felt panic as she stepped into ankle-deep water. Turning on the light in the hall, she saw that the entire floor had 3 inches of water.

Just great, now we are sinking, she thought. Was the boat coming apart in the pounding? She quickly ran for Charlie.

Charlie took one look and knew he needed to get Larry fast. He went outside and was immediately blasted by sheets of sea and rainwater. Using all his might, he held on and made his way up the ladder to the fly bridge. "Larry, we are taking on water. The head and galley floors are full of water," said Charlie with a tense sound in his voice.

As Charlie and Larry went below to find out more, Jim grabbed his microphone, "Henry, this is the Mystic Lady."

Henry had been pouring some coffee. Looking at his watch, he keyed his microphone and said, "A little early, what's up my friend?"

"Well, the good news is that the seas have not built any

higher, the bad is that we are taking on water. Not really sure what it is that has given up. Larry is checking it out now. I realize you can't do much for us, but I wanted to let you know anyway." Jim gave his position to Henry again.

Henry looked at the chart before him, "Humm, you're making good time. You've only got another 18 miles. Relax, you're going to make it. Besides, if you really need us, I'll send in the troops. We have a helicopter crew on stand by at Opa-locka. I've already checked with them and they said it would be tricky, but they could get you out of there." In truth, it would be almost impossible to rescue anyone from a pitching deck in 50 mph winds. Although it had been done, it surely would be no cake-walk.

Jim knew the odds, but tried hard to hang on to the commander's words. On a nice day, 18 miles was nothing. On this bleak and dismal night, it might as well have been 1,000. Jim reached up and hit the "time to go" button on his GPS. At 3.8 knots, it flashed back the time to reach home, 5 hours and 50 minutes.

Remaining calm, Jim tried to remind himself he was already home. This was where he worked, his office with a view. He just did not particularly like the view tonight. It always amazed Jim how quickly the sea could change. Yet in all his life, he had to admit he had never seen her act so angry and unforgiving. One wrong turn of the wheel and these seas would just swallow them up.

As he held the wheel, he began to feel drained and completely exhausted. His eyesight began to blur as he tried hard to remain focused.

"Jim, if you need me, just remember I am here. The storm's forward speed has slowed down some. If it helps, I've done some calculations, and at your present speed it will be close, but you should arrive just ahead of the main force of the storm," boomed the confident and patient voice of Henry.

So this is just the beginning, Jim thought. He could not fathom what it would be like in the full force of the storm. "We made it this far. Thanks for the vote of confidence," was his tired reply.

"Bad news is that the forecasters think she will get even stronger over the warm Gulf Stream if she slows her race across the Atlantic," said Henry.

"Great, hope we're home before landfall. Where do they think the eye wall will pass?" asked Jim.

"It's hard to say exactly, but right now there is an 80 percent chance it will pass right over the Middle Keys," answered Henry.

"You're not making me feel any better. Got any good news?" asked Jim.

"Sure, there is a 20 percent chance they are wrong," answered Henry with a chuckle.

"What time do they think she will make landfall," asked Jim, looking at the time to go display flashing 5 hours and 20 minutes.

"Right now they say she will hit in five hours," answered Henry.

Jim's heart sank. They needed to make up some time. If not, they would be dead for sure. "Henry, it's going to be real close, please let me know if the landfall time changes, I'll let you know what is leaking. This is the Mystic Lady standing by on one six," said Jim.

Below deck, Larry had torn away an access panel, and with a flashlight in his teeth he began inspecting the hull wall. Even without his light, he could immediately hear where the water was rushing in. The through hull fitting for the macerator pump on the toilette storage tank was sheared off due to the force of the pounding.

Thinking quickly, Charlie raced to a storage locker in

the galley. Charlie opened it and removed a heavy-duty industrial pump. Larry had used this pump as an extra live well pump to keep baits alive during tournaments. Charlie needed no more instructions as he hooked up the electric and began pumping out the standing water. The good news was that the three main bilge pumps were also humming right along, but they could not keep up with the water gushing in.

The additional pump gave Larry much-needed breathing room to find a solution. Furiously, he began tearing through drawers in search of something to use as a plug. In the third drawer he found what he needed. In the bottom of a spare tackle drawer lay a huge soft-headed, bullet-shaped, Moldcraft lure Larry had used as a teaser for marlins. It was in the perfect shape of a plug and, being soft, it should fit snugly in the hole. Instinctively he reached for his wire cutters and removed the leader. Rushing back into the head, he loaded up the lure with silicone and positioned the plug in the opening. Fighting the incoming water, he sealed off the hole. Charlie handed him a hammer, and with a few solid strikes, the water slowed and then stopped.

With no more water coming in, Charlie and Larry put their backs against the bulkhead, slid down, and sat down in the water. Embracing one another, they breathed deeply, feeling they had at least for the moment saved the ship.

In another 15 minutes, the remaining water was pumped out. Charlie had kept Jim posted on their progress. Jim got on the radio and called Henry, "Henry, Larry has stopped the water, we still have a fighting chance to make it back."

"That's great, Jim, I'll stand by if anything changes," replied Henry.

Everyone now reverted to feeling ill again. It was amazing that they had actually felt better in the pure panic that followed finding the water.

As Larry was finishing up downstairs, he looked up. One of the cabinets he had earlier searched through was still open. The cabinet door was swinging open and shut wildly in the pitching seas. Inside the teak cabinet, an old demon was rearing its ugly head and beckoning Larry to submit. As the door would swing open and the hinge would creak, Larry was faced with an old companion, half a bottle of bourbon.

Just one long swallow and he would make it through this night of terror. In his mind he could remember the burning sensation the bourbon would make as it touched his lips and ran down his throat. He remembered the warm glowing feeling he had remembered as the alcohol would hit his blood stream and seem to permeate the layers of his skin with a cool numbness.

With the stress he had been through, Larry reached for the bottle. It was an old bottle of "Wild Turkey." Unscrewing the top he could smell the comforting aroma of the alcohol. Just one long swallow, what could it hurt, he thought.

He was about to take a long swallow when suddenly he stopped. Jim might need him. He would need all of him, his judgment could not be impaired. It took great fortitude as he reluctantly screwed the crusty top back on the bottle. He felt his entire body scream with pain as he placed the bottle back on the shelf and he closed the door.

Thankfully for Larry's pride, Ricardo had not witnessed the devil tempting him. Ricardo had taken the chance to use the head before going back up on the bridge. When he was finished, both Ricardo and Larry went back up on the fly bridge to assist Jim in navigating.

Using binoculars in this pitching sea seemed almost

comical, yet Jim had thought he had seen a light just off to port. After trying unsuccessfully, he put the glasses away and said, "I know we are too far out to see Alligator Reef Lighthouse in this stuff, but can you guys make some lights at 10 o'clock?"

Larry and Ricardo strained but could only see rain, foam and water as they scanned ahead. The wind hitting the wave tops almost looked like prop wash from a helicopter, making them almost completely blind.

Feeling the pressure to speed up their progress, Jim decided to start his port engine. Holding his breath momentarily, he let out a sigh as it fired up. Putting the engine in gear, he felt better than he had felt in many hours. There it is again, he thought. "I could swear I just saw a green and white light; could it be a fishing boat out here tonight?" asked Jim.

Ricardo peered into the darkness and just for a second thought he saw it also.

Jim grabbed his radio and gave Henry his position. "Henry, I see something that appears to be getting closer. What are you tracking in our area?"

"I have a tanker last reported 10 miles north of you, and we had that tug pulling a barge, but he has not reported in for over an hour."

As Jim rode up the back of a towering wave before him, all he could see was darkness from the sky above through his windshield. As they began their decent downward, Jim saw with horror a boat directly in front of them and screamed, "Oh shit!" The green and white mast lights could now be clearly seen. The vessel's green port light was also visible. With the momentum of gravity pulling her down the wave, the 15-ton Mystic Lady increased forward speed toward disaster.

Jim was thankful he had only moments before engaged his port engine. Placing both engines in reverse, he increased speed to full throttle. Even above the roar of the storm, the engines made an awkward shudder. He risked a high probability of broaching, but the risk of collision caused him to overrule his natural instincts.

Ricardo and Jim held their breath as even in full reverse the boat continued toward the fishing vessel. It's going to be close, thought Jim as he spun the wheel hard starboard. Even in the ragging sea, the sound of Jim's outrigger colliding with the others ship's rigging could be heard. With a loud clank and a whipping snap the outrigger came loose again and shot back into the side of the Mystic Lady's tower.

With a sigh of relief, Jim realized they had made it. Shining a spotlight back toward the other ship's stern, they could read the name, Beulah Pride. Switching his radio to low power and keying his mike, Jim said, "Beulah Pride, Beulah Pride, Beulah Pride, this is the Mystic Lady, you guys see me almost ram your port side?"

"Ya, I seen ya, good boat handling, skipper. I thought we was dun fur sure. Sorry, I ded not see ya sooner, but dis rain makes for shitty visability. My name is Captain Phillip Debouis. I was hoping to beat dis thing south. Looks lik it ain't gona happen. Where you boys headin?"

"My name is Captain Jim Riley. We are heading back home to Islamorada. We've seen some bad weather, but we're making progress. I think we will make it before the main force blows in. You guys want to follow us in. We have some nice warm coffee waiting."

"No tanks, dough, I'm gona keep headin south. Dis one tough ole boat, we'll be OK. I am soory to say, but at least I feel bedder knowin I am not de only fool out here in dis stuff."

"Fool I am, but I am also glad I'm not by myself, either.

You take care, buddy, and don't hesitate to call if you need a friend."

"Aye, see ya."

And as quickly at the two boats met, they disappeared again in divergent directions. Jim watched as already the Beulah Pride's lights faded into the oppressive darkness.

CHAPTER TWENTY-EIGHT

In the numbness of the past several hours, Jim held a death grip on the wheel and became quite good at handling the heavy seas. The only way to really learn boat handling in these conditions was through experience. With all his years, however, he had never been prepared for a night quite like this.

As exhausted as he was, he became increasingly optimistic. Hell, he had made it this far, how much worse could it get? Best of all, the reef line on his chart plotter was quickly approaching. In normal conditions, Jim could easily cross the reef, with little concern for the depth. In these high seas the crossing would be treacherous.

With walls of water 55 feet tall, running into the shallows of the reef sometimes only 15 feet deep, the crossing would have to be picture perfect.

In almost total darkness, Jim could only trust his plotter and plan to cross at the deepest point he could find. Even then, he would have to plan to cross on the crest of a wave in order to clear the jagged teeth of the coral.

He would plan to cross the reef line about a mile east of Alligator Reef. Just past a wreck called the "Eagle," the reef formed what looked like a funnel on the chart. Locals called it the "North Hole." It was here that Jim would try to jump the reef. To himself, Jim wished he could at least have some moonlight in which to see. Everything looked so bleak in the pitch-black night.

At a snail's pace, the distance to go continued to decrease. Both Larry and Ricardo were on deck when they could for the first time actually see lights from the Keys. "Home's never looked so good," said Larry as a smile actually came across his face.

"To me this is a vision I have dreamed about often, yet it still feels so far away," said Ricardo to the other two on the fly bridge.

Voice traffic on the radio had quieted down in the past few hours. All but a very few boats had long settled in or moved clear of the area. As Jim keyed his microphone, he felt as if he and the Coast Guard would be the only people listening. "Coast Guard Station Islamorada, this is the Mystic Lady, over," said Jim.

"Read you loud and clear, Jim. What's your location?" came Henry's steady deep voice.

"'Bout a half mile off the Eagle. The rain has actually picked up, but we can see some lights from shore. Sure looks welcoming," answered Jim

Like piping-hot coffee on a cold winter morning, Henry's voice boomed, "We're waiting with open arms, my friend. We've cleared a spot for you beside the station canal. I knew you would make it, if you hurry you should be tied up about 15 minutes before the first hurricane band hits, you really picked up some speed!"

"Yeah, that Gulf Stream was really screaming north tonight. Sure was lucky so far; hopefully, we will see you soon. Thanks for the dock space, we could never make the hurricane hole tonight," said Jim. "We'll call when we get close to Snake Creek."

In the Keys, everyone with a boat the size of Jim's had a hurricane hole. It was usually a spot on the bay side surrounded by mangroves. The boats are tied off on all points and put in the middle of a little basin. In a hurricane evacuation, the bridges will not open for boat traffic after a designated time. The Snake Creek bridge is the only bridge north of the Seven Mile Bridge that Jim could possibly fit under with the bridge down. Even so, Larry would have to climb in the tower and lower antennas and the canvas top in order to give the boat enough clearance.

Under these unusually high tides, Jim might even have to take a hack saw to his precious tower in order to pass. He would do it if necessary, but only as a last resort.

"Coast Guard Station Islamorada, this is the Beulah Pride, over," came a tense voice over the radio. Captain Debouis resisted calling the Coast Guard as long as possible. With no other shrimpers around, he felt he owed it to the crew to at least call in his position.

"This is Coast Guard Islamorada, switch and answer on 22 alpha, Beulah Pride," said Henry.

Everyone with a radio, including Jim, hurried to their set and switched over to 22A to hear what was going on with the Beulah Pride. The somber, serious tone with a French accent spelled trouble and anyone listening could sense it.

"Coast Guard Station, this is Captain Philip Debouis. We have been barely making way. We are heading south trying to outrun the storm. The Gulf Stream appears to be moving north very fast tonight, we are barely making two knots. We are 12 miles out and taking a beating. We are not taking on water, but I wanted you to know our exact position at 24.59.27 North and 080.34.82 West. We are a shrimp boat out of Louisiana. We should be OK, just wanted to let you know we were out here," said Philip.

"Glad to hear you're hanging in there, Beulah Pride, we

will begin tracking you. The main force of the storm is fast approaching. If you haven't already, recommend you put bow to the wind and ride her out from here. You're not going to make any headway into this current," responded Henry.

"We will do that," answered Phillip. "We have our sleds in the water for extra stability. I will advise you if we are in distress." The sleds, usually used to rake the ocean's bottom and keep the nets separated, were lowered just under the water's surface in rough weather, reducing the vessel's side-to-side roll.

Looking down at his instruments, Philip smiled a faint smile. At least the diesel engine had not forsaken him, it was purring like a kitten. The barometer however, had been steadily falling more than a millibar every hour. Philip needed no weather forecaster to know that as pressure drops the winds rush in to replace the low-pressure vacuum.

"Beulah Pride, this is the Mystic Lady, over," said Jim.

"Ya got me brodder, want go to 69," Philip replied.

Jim switched his set over to channel 69 and said, "You all right, friend? You sound a little flustered."

"We hanging in der. It's getting pretty ugly, dough."

"We can see lights from home, sure you don't want to head this way?"

"No I jus have ta wait it out, brodder. We'll be OK. Danks for the encouragement. Beulah Pride will be standing by on one six."

"You hang in there, buddy. If you need any words of encouragement, I am here. You just keep that pointy thing pointed into them waves, she'll hold together," Jim told Phillip. To himself he thought, nothing is going to hold together in these seas and, damn, it's only gonna get worse. Jim could hear the tenseness in the other man's voice. Even as fearless as Phillip sounded, he knew he was looking at death thumping on his old hull.

Over the past couple of hours, the wind had also been clocking steadily around with the approaching storm. The breeze the past few days had been out of the East. At 8 p.m. the wind increased in speed and began moving clockwise to the southeast, the south, the west and then for two hours it began wailing from the North.

To experienced seamen, an anemometer is not needed to judge wind speed on a fishing vessel. When wind speed hits 40 knots, the ship's rigging begins to scream. To the inexperienced, it sounds like a baby in desperate need of its mother.

By 9:30, the cables began to shriek like demons in a horror movie. To the crew, they knew the wind speed had now exceeded 50 miles per hour. The seas began to grow exponentially higher with each increase in wind velocity.

How Philip had not foreseen the Gulf Stream current was an unforgivable faux pas. He pictured his late father's face admonishing him for such a rookie blunder. It would be a long night, but he had been in storms before. As long as he had power, he could handle anything, he thought.

Just then a huge rogue wave crashed 60 feet over the bow, submerging the deck and wheelhouse under several tons of water. A rogue wave is one out of pattern from the rest. It is much larger, and usually from a slightly different angle than the others. It is impossible to plan for, and one rogue wave alone could easily sink a ship.

As water poured through her scrubbers, the air in the hull created positive buoyancy, thrusting her back toward the surface. Anything in the wall of water's path had been flattened. The worst damage was to the antennas. The wave sheared off all the antennas from the wheelhouse.

With no VHF radio, loran and global positioning system, the Beulah Pride was both dumb and blind. Captain Philip could only point her into the waves now and wait for daylight. To himself he thought, what a long, lonely damn night it was going to be.

The winds then began to once again shift. Intensifying once more, the gale began blowing from the Northeast, and the rigging actually began to moan. To ancient mariners, when the rigging moaned, it was taken as a song of warning from a goddess. To most it foretold, like some age-old song, that their death was near. To the crew on the Beulah Pride, it meant that the wind speeds were bumping hurricane force.

In 1805, Adm. Sir Francis Beaufort, working for the British Royal Navy, developed the Beaufort Wind Scale. He developed a table for various sea conditions in order to determine how much canvas a fully rigged frigate could carry. In doing so, he created a table of wave heights in relation to wind speed. With the rigging moaning, the wind had surpassed 11 on the Beaufort scale. At 12 on the scale, the wind speed was 74 to 82 miles per hour and the seas would be over 14 meters or 46 feet in height.

The crew on the Beulah Pride had no choice but to try to remain calm. The captain's brother-in-law, Jean Matise, headed below to the engine room. If the engine failed, their fate would be sealed for sure. Jean stood by with spare fuel filters and a full assortment of tools. With all the turbulence, the tank's bottom would stir up 30 years of sludge. If the motor started sputtering, he would be ready.

Clayton Jones remained in the wheelhouse with Capt. Philip Debouis. Bracing themselves with every crashing wave, it was a ride from hell. The cook, Pierre Bonnard, and David Jacques-Louise went below to the sleeping quarters. Privately imploding from the pressure, Pierre went for his stash of pot and they lit up a joint. The two men began laughing hysterically as they began to get stoned.

Back on the Mystic Lady, working both spotlights, Ricardo and Larry could see for the first time the fury of the water crushing the reef before them. "We'll never make it! We've got to turn back!" said Larry with sudden panic in his voice.

"Sorry, friend, it's our only hope. Better go below and make sure everyone has their life jackets on," said Jim.

"Will do, be right back," said Larry as he gripped the wet rail tightly and climbed down below. In the main cabin, John had everything under control. Larry quickly explained to him what lay ahead. John wasted no time getting everyone ready for the worst-case scenario.

Jim could feel the waves bunching up as they encountered the increasingly shallow waters of the reef. He began to judge his timing and plan his crossing. Licking his lips, he tasted the salt that had accumulated in his mustache. Finally gritting his teeth, he increased his throttle and rode the back of a wave across the beginning of the reef. Increasing his speed, he laid just behind the crest as the boat was tossed like a toy into the white foam before them.

Jim could barely hold the wheel as they were pummeled across the shallows as if they were on a small raft on a white water rapid. Ricardo was on the floor, and Larry had struck his head on the piping. A sharp clang was heard from deep in the ship's innards. It sounded terrible and for a moment Jim thought they had grounded. Then the old girl climbed up out of the hole and kept moving. Jim could feel a bad vibration transmitted through his steering wheel.

Studying all of his instruments, everything looked normal. Taking pause, he waited, expectant of a bilge pump automatically going off, revealing a gaping hole in the hull. Nothing happened; they just kept sliding over the shallows. Thank God, only a dinged prop. Thank you, sweet Jesus, Jim thought. Bleeding from his forehead, Larry looked up and said, "We made it!" He put an arm around Jim and yelled at the top of his lungs. "We actually made it!" They all felt victorious.

With the reef acting as a giant buffer, the seas were much more bearable once on the inside. Pointing the nose of the Mystic Lady for the mid-channel marker at Snake Creek on his chart plotter, Jim increased throttle and made his way toward home. The vibration got worse. It could be disastrous, but with the time factor he was forced to push it.

Now running Hawk Channel, Jim might as well have been in a harbor. The seas were still running 6 to 8. On a bad day of fishing, this would still be considered nasty offshore. The rain had not let up, but Jim relaxed and lit a cigar. Exhaling deliberately, he began to relax and grow more confident. From here it should be a cakewalk.

Trusting his instruments, he continued toward the heading on his GPS. Not seeing the flashing beacon of the marker was uncomfortable but understandable in this driving rain. "It's going to get bumpy in the channel. On a good day it is only 5 feet deep at the No. 1 marker," yelled Jim.

"Yeah, going to have to ride another wave in," said Larry.

Pointing, Ricardo said, "Look, there, flashing white, must be our marker."

Waiting for another quick flash, Jim acknowledged and said, "Good eyes, Ricardo, you found it!" Jim continued on autopilot until a hundred yards off the marker. Just then a huge bolt of lightning hit the water 200 yards off the bow. The sky and water lit up before them, turning the shallow water a bluish white. Being so close, the sound of the thunder was both instant and deafening. Crisp static electricity filled the air.

The crew exchanged looks of both awe and utter fear. Each passenger was thankful for the lightning missing the boat. Switching off the autopilot, Jim took the wheel again. Larry began searching with the spotlight and found the next unlit green reflective marker. These markers will be history in just a few hours, he thought.

The rules for navigating a channel were easy to remember. When returning from sea, a simple phrase keeps you on the correct side of the marker. As Jim approached the marker, being exhausted and badly in need of rest, even he quietly muttered it to himself, "red right return." The saying "red right return" means that you must keep the red marker on the right side of your boat when returning from sea. Therefore you pass the green on your left. Jim knew this channel in his sleep, but tonight it looked like a foreign port he was entering for the very first time.

With the help of the spotlight, the red reflector tape on the red marker also illuminated. Because he felt so fatigued, Jim tried to envision himself as a football, traveling between two goal posts, as he positioned his boat in the middle of the two reflective markers. With the crazy seas, harrowing wind and blinding rain, what should be routine was actually quite intricate.

His fatigued mind went back to the Orange Bowl. He thought of all the Florida State field goals against the University of Miami, wide right. Not tonight, he thought, this time he would hold the wheel and slide right through. Judging the waves rolling on the approaching flat, he again increased his throttle and rode the back of an approaching one. He felt the boat pulling hard to the right as the markers were just off the bow. It took all his tenacity to keep the bow between the markers and pass cleanly in between.

Three points, he thought to himself, as he safely entered the more protected channel. Snake Creek was named snake for a reason. It is shaped just like a winding snake. But even with the driving rain, the creek would be easy compared to what the crew had just been through. The waters in the creek were the calmest they had felt since leaving Cay Sal.

Ricardo took over spotlight duty, as Larry climbed up the tower to reduce their clearance under the bridge. Making the final turn, Jim pointed the bow under the bridge. Reading the vertical clearance marker at the bridge entrance with the spotlight, it read 48 feet. Taking a deep breath, he realized that with Larry reducing their clearance 5 feet, they should make it. It would be a tough right turn after passing under the bridge. Rocks would be on both sides with the stiff wind hitting them broadside. Larry gave the all clear, and Jim got back on the radio.

Ignoring radio protocol, Jim said, "Henry, we're home. We'll be at the docks in a few minutes."

"See you in a few, Jim," boomed Henry. Approaching the bridge, Larry remained up top. He would make the call if they had to turn back quickly if the marker was wrong, and they were not going to have enough clearance. Jim was lucky it was still low tide.

Jim felt better when Larry yelled at the top of his lungs, "All clear, Jim, you got it. Take us home."

Increasing throttle slightly to maintain steerage, Jim felt satisfied as he passed under the bridge. He banked hard starboard to make the canal on their right. Once in the protected water of the canal, the feeling was serene. Docking at the Coast Guard Station, Jim wanted to leave the boat and head directly for Linda at home. If anything had happened to her, he would never be able to forgive himself.

From under the lower level of the Coast Guard Station a figure came running toward them in the driving rain. Squinting through his exhausted eyes, Jim recognized the silhouette of the figure approaching. "Linda, is that you?" he asked.

"It's me, Jim," answered Linda, like a parent arriving at school to pick up a misbehaving youngster. "You really had me worried, hope you have a damn good reason," she answered calmly but with coldness in her voice.

"Linda, I don't know what to say. I went on a mission. It was top secret and I could not tell you the plan. We really did something great, though. We rescued several people from the jaws of communism. We also stopped a bully from being able to flex his muscles for a very long time. It was a long, lonely ride out there tonight. I had a lot of time to think. I realize just how much you mean to me. I don't know how to start all over, but I know that if we put the past behind us, we just might make it into the future, Linda," said Jim, reaching out for her in the pouring rain. "I love you, baby, do you forgive me, do you forgive me for everything?"

Salty tears intermixed with the rain as they embraced.

"Jim, I also had some time to think. I thought for a little while that you just might not be coming back tonight! I pictured all kinds of horrible things happening to you out there. I just don't know what my life would be like without you. Honey, I didn't like it. I'm also sorry. I know I've been so jealous of what you've been doing. I know I've held my anger with more regard than my love for you. Let's start over tonight, I love you, baby," said Linda, placing her tender forehead on the crook of his shoulder and neck.

On deck Charlie kept an eye on the scientist and the

Cuban intelligence officer. Ricardo and Ana looked around in awe and disbelief. They had actually made it! They were standing on United States soil! Their dream had come true. Here they were in the land they had dreamed of. With absolutely no concern for the storm still bearing down on them they also kissed and hugged one another.

Jim made his way to the Coast Guard station office. Climbing the flight of stairs and entering the duty station, "Anybody got a hot cup of coffee 'round here?" asked Jim.

"Made a fresh pot when you made Snake Creek, Jim," answered Henry dressed in his Coast Guard whites.

Putting an arm around Henry, Jim said, "Henry, I can't tell you what it meant to have you on the radio with me tonight. I don't think I could have kept a level head and made it home without you."

"Just doing my job, Captain," said Henry a bit shyly.

"Have you heard from that boat, Beulah Pride, in a while?" asked Jim.

"No, sure haven't. That captain sure sounded like he had his hands full." Walking over to the other officer sitting by the radio Henry said, "Skally, try and raise Beulah Pride, will you?"

"Aye, Aye, Commander. Beulah Pride, Beulah Pride, Beulah Pride, this is Coast Guard Station Islamorada, do you copy? Over," asked Skally. Waiting three minutes for a reply, he tried again several more times. They never got a response. The silence on the radio smelled of trouble.

"Doesn't look good for 'em," said Henry.

"Well, God willing, they are just too damn busy to chat. Hope that ol' boat is holding together," said Jim.

"I'll notify the Miami group if we still can't reach them in an hour."

"Henry, you're going to have a tough time swallowing this, but we weren't exactly on a fishing trip. You're one of the few people around here that knows my background in the military. Well, Henry, we just came back from Cuba. We were on a mission sanctioned by the highest levels of our government. This thing was so sensitive that if we needed backup, in their eyes it really never happened."

"What are you talking about, Jim, you really do need some sleep," answered Henry.

"No, Henry, I really need your help. On board my vessel are two VIP prisoners from the land of sugar cane. I need you to at least detain them for me until after the storm. The chubby one here is harmless. He is a scientist. We let him roam freely on board. Scar face is the dangerous one. Be careful with him. I'm sure the Navy spooks will fly them out of here as soon as this thing blows over.

"I know this place has seen its fair share of hurricanes, but I saw my place being built. We also have our dog at home. If you don't mind, we'll go back to my house and wait this out there. Can you watch them, Henry?" asked Jim.

Seeing the sincerity in Jim's eyes, Henry said, "Anything you need, we'll take care of it. We have a couple of cells in the back for weekend drunks. It'll work perfectly."

"Just please keep this between us until this blows over. It will all become crystal clear then," said Jim.

Jim left and a few minutes later came back with two prisoners. Henry could tell just by looking that the guy leading them in was also Special Forces. Charlie had the look of a soldier as he followed Henry and placed the men in separate cells. "This should hold them nicely," said Charlie to Jim.

As Henry closed the doors, a heavy metal-to-metal thud could be heard as the doors locked solidly in place. The cells were on the second level, so they would be safe from the tidal surge that was expected any time. With the prisoners safely behind bars, the crew could now focus on securing the Mystic Lady.

Larry went below and brought up all the spare dock lines. He and Jim began cutting off 50-foot sections of anchor line to increase the holding power. The idea was to place the boat in the middle of the canal. Attaching numerous dock lines on both sides of the canal, they would place her right in the center. They began tying the lines at angles in order to act as spring lines. This way, the ship could perhaps survive the 15- to 18-foot tidal surge. With Larry on one side of the canal and Jim on the other, everyone pitched in.

Almost ceremoniously Jim reached down and gave a final tug on a dock line. Smiling, he looked up, "Looks like a damn spider web. If she does go, at least we can tell Liberty Mutual we gave her our best," said a relaxed and totally exhausted Jim.

With the boat secure, all that was left was to go home and lie low. They all crammed into the Ford Expedition and headed south to their home. They were a sorry-looking lot, all soaked to the bone. They had the look of a pack of pathetic dogs that had been left out in the cold and rain.

CHAPTER TWENTY-NINE

Pulling onto US 1, they could see that the well-traveled overseas highway was deserted. In driving rain with gale-force winds, the street signs violently waved their danger signal. The entire Keys were under a mandatory evacuation order and locals were long gone. The wind was howling now and buffeting the Expedition with rain like bullets, as feeder bands of hurricane-force winds steadily turned up their velocity.

Thankfully, the island still had power, but for how long remained to be seen. As they crossed Whale Harbor Bridge and looked left at the two resorts, all the boats, cars and people had disappeared. It looked like a place Jim had never seen before - eerily vacant, expectant.

As they arrived at their street, they pulled in and drove down the tree-lined drive. Jim realized that tomorrow everything would change. Silently he prayed that the storm would suddenly turn north, like so many others. He hoped they would be spared from the unforgiving main thrust of the storm, but in his gut he knew differently. He was thankful that, unlike so many others, he had actually prepared.

During the last few minutes of the ride, everyone in the car remained quiet. Each person silently internalized the power of the storm around them.

"All we can do now is batten down the hatches, make sure the generator cranks up and get settled in for a night of pure hell," said Jim in a dry, tired tone.

"Well, we've taken all she could throw our way so far, how much worse could it get?" said Larry.

"Oh, it will get nasty," said Jim.

"I've moved everything I could lift to save upstairs and, thanks to electric shutters, all the windows are protected," said Linda. As they got out of the car, Jim looked around.

The mango tree he had planted four years ago had just begun to bear fruit. To his left was the royal poinciana Linda had spent all day picking out in the nursery fields up in Homestead. Then there was his favorite palm down by the water. He could not remember how many hours he had spent sitting under that tree sorting out life's mysteries. To himself he wondered how it would all look tomorrow. He felt his stomach lurch as he battled the wind and rain and followed the others up the stairs and entered the warm, dry house up on stilts.

It was 1:35 in the morning when the first severe band of Hurricane Diana approached the Florida Keys. They could watch on TV as it came steadily closer. Like a swipe from an angry Mother Nature, the band came ashore. Watching the radar image with weatherman Bryan Norcross from Channel 4, he explained that things were going to get rough in the Middle and Upper Keys during the next few minutes.

As if on cue, the lights began to flicker. Fierce vertical sheets of rain pounded the north side of the building. The rain came at such force than even with all the doors and windows closed tightly, water broke through the barrier and began entering the house through every orifice.

Charlie put an arm around Maria as Jim and Linda delayed the inevitable and tried to keep up with the incoming water with a mop and towel. Ricardo and Ana sat in the living room and fell asleep huddled together on a soft couch. Staring through the fan-shaped window above the front door, Linda said, "Jim, what's that? Blue lights are flashing all over!"

"It's the transformers exploding all up and down the highway," said Jim.

The smaller power lines failed first. As winds gusted to speeds above 100 miles per hour, the lines were ripped from the poles by flying projectiles propelled through the air. It was only a matter of time before the house would be engulfed in deep darkness. As the power went out, the clutter of noise from the TV also stopped. In total darkness, the havoc of the storm engulfed them.

"Quick, turn on a flashlight," said Linda to Jim. Jim reached for the light he had placed at his side in preparation for this loss of power and turned it on.

The room was now illuminated in the bright but narrow beam of the flashlight. With nothing left to do, Jim and Linda sat down with Charlie and Maria on the floor in an interior hallway. Leaning his back against the wall and sitting on the floor, Jim took his lover's hand as exhaustion overtook him. Jim fell into a deep sleep.

Linda had wanted Jim to stay awake, but knew he had reached his threshold. John just sat down against the hallway wall and felt an inner peace. Although not out of harm's way, he was free again. Regardless of the circumstances, he felt warm and satisfied.

Silently they sat there on the floor. Charlie found a battery- powered radio and turned it on. As they listened to Diana's progression, they sat together and prayed that the protective home would hold together.

The wind advanced in very defined bands. As if Mother

Nature had a hidden accelerator switch, the wind would suddenly increase with the arrival of a new wind band. Almost predictably the wind would howl and whine, sounding remarkably like a jet engine throttling up. As the wind speed peaked, they could feel the concrete bricks of the house shudder as if ready to explode. With the pressure so low outside the structure, everyone's ears began to pop, equalizing the pressure. Then just when they thought the entire place would blow apart, the winds would begin slowing, preparing for the next band.

In the hall, everyone registered relief; they had made it through another band. They held hands and began to breathe again. Their eyes reflected the terror they had just experienced. Linda had never before felt so tense.

Outside, the expected tidal surge came ashore swiftly and with great force. From above, the house looked as if it were in the middle of a raging river. Huge waves of water quashed everything in their path. The royal poinciana, along with almost everything else on Jim and Linda's property, was uprooted and pushed instantaneously across the highway and into the bay. Their Ford Expedition tumbled violently in the powerful current, eventually ending up in the bay and becoming another artificial reefs. Unbeknownst to them, everything Jim and Linda had worked so hard to create in the way of landscaping was being decimated remorselessly in one frenzied moment.

For Capt. Philip Debouis and the crew of the Beulah Pride, the night had become one of a living hell. At this point, simply trying to survive became an increasingly difficult challenge. The seas astonishingly continued to grow even higher. Riding up waves as high as 70 feet became utterly terrifying. With their bow to the wind, it was at times impossible for Philip to determine the actual direction of the wave tops before him.

With Beulah Pride's forward spotlights illuminated, the

sea before them appeared as foam mountains with peaks from differing angles. To mariners, this is what is called "confused seas." No one constant wave direction could be distinguished.

According to naval architects, ships should withstand wave heights in a beam sea equal to the ship's actual beam or width before tending to capsize. This, of course, varies by a vessel's center of gravity. For this reason even with Beulah Pride's beam of 19 feet, 6 inches, she would not last long taking waves on her side. Heaving to, which is pointing the bow into wind, was the only reasonable thing that Captain Debouis could possibly do.

Captain Debouis, for the first time in his career, had stopped looking at his non-functioning navigational equipment or even his compass. His position and progress was irrelevant; he was simply trying to persevere the bleak night. With each tense moment behind him, after years at sea, he had thought himself unflappable. Now wave heights continued to increase. The probability of pitchpoling became a grave concern.

Again, according to naval architects, a vessel should be able to withstand head seas equal to hull length before the probability of flipping stern over bow, or pitchpoling, can happen. Captain Debouis tried to shake it off, but the fear of pitchpoling had a grip on him.

"Better shift sum more fuel aft," said Captain Philip to Clayton Jones, standing watch with him on the bridge.

With a stern nod, Clayton carefully made his way down below to the engine room.

In the bottom of the boat, the creaking and shuddering of the Beulah Pride was magnified by the buffeting water surrounding the hull. To Clayton, the rumblings sounded as if they were on some wild ride through the innards of an angry whale about to be ejected at any moment. Trying to clear his mind and hold back the nausea,

Clayton took a deep breath and entered the wildly shifting engine room.

Jean Matise was soaked in sweat and grease. The hot, heavy air had a caustic, oily smell to it. With the hatchways closed tight, it was at least 110 degrees in the engine room.

"We've got to move more fuel from the bow tanks to the stern. Captain feels her wanting to go over bow first," said Clayton.

Turning the necessary valves, Jean started the pumps moving more fuel aft.

Looking at Jean, Clayton could tell he was about to pass out from the heat and fumes. "Take a break for a while, go up top and cool down," said Clayton.

"Jus keep changing dem filters, don't let the fire go out, boy," said a thankful yet exhausted Jean Matise. The Beulah Pride had two sets of fuel filters, split by a Y valve. In this way, a valve was turned, directing fuel to the backup filter, and filters could be changed with the engine running. Captain Phillip had installed the backup for just this type of situation.

Alone, Clayton could feel the sphincter muscle in his larynx tighten. He could not be at a worse place on the ship if something catastrophic happened.

Back on the bridge, putting an arm around his brother-in-law, Jean Matise forced a small smile. "You really got us in sum shit now, brodder."

"Yeah, we gona make it, though. She one tough bitch," answered Captain Debouis.

It was then that a possible catastrophe struck its deadly blow. A huge wall of water, towering just over 100 feet, grudgingly started lifting the bow up the steep wall of water. The ship's forward progress almost stopped entirely, as she shuddered and labored to reach the peak of the crest. Suddenly the bottom fell out from under her and the two men standing in the tiny bridge saw absolutely nothing before them. It was as if they fell into a black hole that had opened before them in the ocean.

As the Beulah Pride descended, it was a horrific sight to be sure. She was almost completely vertical, her bow pointing down, her props spun wildly above, in search of some water to bite into. To the men on the Beulah, the free fall felt like an eternity.

As the bow crashed into the water below them, the next wave took the bow under, and forced it deep. The stern then flipped, end over end. The 68-foot vessel now looked like a toy boat in a bathtub, being tossed about like a tiny ball batted around by a kitten.

The entire crew hung precariously upside down for several seconds that seemed to drag on for minutes. As lights throughout the ship began to flicker and then pop off, hope was quickly fading among the crew.

With water pouring into the bridge, Capt. Debouis said, "Come on, baby, come on, baby, let's not end it like this. Right yourself, right yourself, Goddamn it!"

As if the heart and soul of the old ship obediently pulled herself together for one last command, the capsized shrimp boat began to rise up with another large wave. With the tug of gravity from her heavy keel, the Beulah Pride tediously began to right herself.

As they sat upright, the disoriented captain took his place once more at the helm. Looking at the gauges, he yelled, "We did it!" and pounded his clinched fist on top of the wheel.

The RPM gauge indicated that miraculously the motor was still burning diesel. Capt. Debouis instinctively spun the wheel in order to head back into the sea.

Just as relief was beginning to set in, disaster once again struck. The rigging on the starboard, having exceeded its stress limits, suddenly cracked and fell off the right side of the boat. As the rigging hit the deck, on its way toward the water, a fracture in the wooden hull opened up like an anchovy can.

As the floundering lopsided vessel began to heel heavily toward the starboard, the Beulah Pride was now unjustly at the mercy of the whipped-up fury around it. As the waves began to pile up on her port side, the old boat began listing badly.

Each wave now was acting like a giant sledgehammer, pounding her farther and farther over on her side. At this point, the crew was powerless to do anything. They could only hold on and hope for the best. Almost unceremoniously, the Beulah Pride once more capsized.

This time there would be no possible recovery. The crew's only remaining hope was to try to escape as expeditiously as possible. With the boat once again upside down, the seas began lacerating her to bits. The Beulah Pride paid her ultimate price. In a matter of minutes she became just another statistic. She would be listed as one of over a thousand ships to have her final resting place in the bottom of the Straits of Florida.

The first man to die was Jean Matise. With the impact, Jean went head first though the bridge window. The impact alone most likely killed him. He was ejected and never seen again.

In the sleeping quarters, the cook, Pierre Bonnard, and David Jacques-Louise were slammed into the bulkhead. They could hear water rushing in from every direction. Totally disoriented and now completely in the dark, they were not sure which way was up.

In all their previous voyages, no one had ever put forth a plan to get out of an upside-down vessel in utter darkness. Feeling their way, they somehow got separated. Pierre headed toward the wheelhouse. David followed his natural tendency and climbed up, but was actually heading toward the ship's bilge.

The Beulah Pride was now going down quick. Opening a bulkhead, Pierre was abruptly overcome by the force of water that followed. Pinning him in a hallway, he began flailing against the oncoming water, but could make no headway. Quickly expending both his air and energy, he realized he had no chance. This made him try all the more desperately. Kicking and swimming he blacked out, never reaching the surface.

Reaching the engine room, Clayton could hear David's scream of panic. "Calm down, boy, we gona get outa here," called out Clayton.

Knowing that he had no chance to fight his way to the deck, Clayton had decided to stay put. At least here, there was an air pocket. For how long remained to be seen. Maybe help would arrive, but most likely he would just live a few more minutes instead of drowning trying to fight his way out in darkness.

"You went the wrong way, Davie," said Clayton.

Searching in the dark, the two men embraced one another, standing on what once was the engine room ceiling.

Capt. Philip Debouis could see his end coming, and there was not a damn thing he could do about it. The force of the crashing boat destroyed the wheelhouse. The entire bridge controls had been pushed back into a bulkhead. Captain Debouis was now hopelessly pinned between the wheel and a wall. Try as he might, he could not free himself. All he could do now was wait for his death to come.

Upside down, 30 feet deep, in total darkness, he first began to pray. Angry, he then stopped. How could I have let this happen! Sorry, dad, I know I really let you down, he thought. With one final burst of energy he tried one last time to free himself, severely lacerating the palm of his right hand.

With magnanimous determination he closed his eyes

and fought the urge to breathe. Captain Philip's blood was beginning to starve for fresh oxygen. He could hear his pulse rate pound in his temples as his blood became saturated in carbon dioxide. Philip could sense a tunnel closing as he longed for one more breath of fresh air.

Please just one more breath of air, he pleaded. It now became a war of willpower. His brain told him to inhale, his willpower told him to hold off breathing in water.

Finally his brain involuntarily won over. His mouth opened, his lungs, like his Beulah Pride, abruptly filled with saltwater. It was only a matter of time now. One circuit at a time in Philip's body began to silently shut down. His eyes were still open when death began to take over. What remaining oxygen he had in his blood went to his brain. His loneliness and darkness was gradually replaced with a warm bright light. As he slowly lost consciousness, the feelings he had only moments ago of terror and agony were replaced with a sense of peace and tranquility.

As the ship's weight pulled the ship downward, the air still trapped in the hull fought to keep her on the surface. In normal circumstances, a boat like this could remain floating upside down this way for many days. In the storm, however, with tons of water crashing over the keel, things slowly started coming apart. The main beam, a 6-by-6 timber, began to buckle and shift sideways. This caused outer planks to loosen their seal.

As planks began to break up, water started to seep, then pour in. For Clayton and David, what remaining air existed would soon be displaced by salt water. When just enough structural integrity was exhausted, a main support beam collapsed violently. What took place next was both cataclysmic to the boat and liberating for the men huddled in the hull.

As the boat began descending more rapidly now, an entire section of planks just below the engine room gave way. One moment they had given up all hope, and in the next they were expelled into the cool water. They were propelled back up to the frothy surface on a burst of air forced up out of the hull by the surrounding water pressure.

Nearly drowned from the experience, both men coughed up seawater once on the surface. Only 30 feet separated them, but it might as well have been miles in the dark foam-filled air. Debris from the wreckage was scattered over an acre of ocean. Both men found different pieces of timber and held on tightly.

Their only remaining chance of survival had already been deployed. As designed, the eight-man life raft had automatically ejected earlier, as the water sensitive switch activated the air canister. The EPIRB attached to the raft had also determined something was amiss and began transmitting a distress signal to a satellite high up above.

Clayton first saw the flashing strobe light on top of the raft. Continuing to hold on to a plank, he kicked his way through the raging surf and took hold of the raft. Climbing in, he hit the floor of the raft and collapsed. A few moments later, David, also attracted to the flashing strobe, joined him.

With no sense of direction, the two men had no idea that the winds had switched direction almost an hour earlier. The main furry of the storm for them had passed. With each passing band of wind, the next became measurably more bearable.

Several times over the next hour, the raft carried up the crest of a wave, caught the wind and tumbled down the steep other side, flipping end over end. Clayton and David had no choice, but to strap themselves in and right the raft once it stabilized.

The Coast Guard station in Islamorada was built in 1968. Although there are tougher building codes today, back then most structures were built solidly. It was not worth a contractor's reputation to cut corners. Even though the station was built like a fortress from top to bottom, Diana began to take a toll on the old building. Water, which was forced over the highway US 1, really picked up speed as it passed over the elevated highway and struck the building. The raised roadway acted like a rock in a stream. All around it, the current screamed. The southern wall happened to be the wall protecting the prison cells containing Ernesto Gonzalez and Major Javier Suarez.

The trip over had been hellish enough for both men. Being locked up in cells with only nominal emergency lighting and the storm pounding away outside had driven the two men into solemn silence. Each man retreated into opposite corners of his adjoining cell. Ernesto's overweight thighs were too large to cross, so he sat on the floor with his feet extended straight out before him. Javier sat with a look of utter discontent on his face, his legs and arms crossed before him.

With absolutely no warning the wall directly behind Javier failed. The sound of crumbling concrete could not be heard over the sound of the water rushing in and sweeping Javier and the entire contents of his cell into the torrent below. Ernesto winced hearing the long scream from Javier as he grabbed for his foam mattress and was swept into the maelstrom below.

Ernesto knew he would be next. He sat in the corner and wept, ready for his wall to also collapse at any time. Tonight, good luck was on his side. Although many times during the next few hours it felt as if the entire structure would blow apart, remarkably until now he had been spared. Somehow the rest of the old building held together.

It had been three hours since the first band had come ashore. Unexpectedly, the winds dropped and then quit blowing altogether. "Thank you, God, we made it," said Ana in Spanish looking up toward the heavens.

"You mean to say, we have made it this far," answered Charlie. "The eye wall has just come ashore. Depending on its location, we could have about 15 minutes of peace before the winds change direction. The other side of the storm will hit with the same intensity, or greater than our last band, so hold on," said Charlie.

Everyone says not to do it, but still they could not resist the temptation. With much trepidation, they slowly opened the front door. Jim had awakened now.

"Looks like the place held together so far. Hope she can handle the second half," said Jim.

"Holy cow," said Linda as she looked below with the flashlight. She did not recognize what she saw below them. Everything was flat. To herself, she was hoping that maybe it was due to the starkness of the nighttime. Everything looked different at night, she had tried to reassure herself.

After seeing what used to be their yard below them, it amazed even Jim that the house had actually held together. This was a killer storm, he thought as he wondered how many had been killed tonight. Silently, he said a prayer asking for the Lord to watch over his friends and family. Would God have brought me this far, only to perish in this house?

Without warning, and with tremendous power, the eastern eye wall slammed into them. As if on cue, the wind began to shriek, only this time pounding the southern side of their home. With nothing else to do, everyone once more took up a position in the hallway. With fearful eyes, they held hands. This time their eyes held a different kind of fear, no longer a look fearing the unknown; it was a look of dread, knowing what was about to happen, unable to control it, praying to survive it.

"The one positive thing is that from here on out, it will only get better. Each band will now be weaker than the previous one," said Jim.

"Yeah, same drill as before, only in reverse order," replied Larry.

It was as if Mother Nature was playing a cruel joke. She

had pounded everything from the north with winds exceeding 180 miles per hour. What little that had defied falling over or being uprooted had survived only sparingly. Now with winds of equal strength, from an opposite direction, little could persevere this double whammy. Material that had been blown and pushed across the highway now made its way back. Only this time, nature had stepped on it, kicked it and pounded it with all its force, like an angry, perverse child.

For several more hours the storm raged on. Gradually, everyone realized that they had made it. There was a distinct difference in the wind. It was still blowing outside, but the intensity was not there. Hurricane Diana was winding down, at least in the Florida Keys.

With a green light from the Miami Coast Guard group a rescue helicopter was dispatched from Opa-locka Airport. With only a slight amount of light over the eastern horizon, they waited for the safety officer to give the OK to begin a search.

Smokey Joe Davis was an old Australian bush pilot. He had spent many years of his early career shuffling various cargos to distant villages all over the Ivory Coast of Africa. Because of his uncanny knowledge of the local areas, he was talked into signing on with Southern Air Transport, flying in relief aid to the war-torn country of Angola.

To this day, Smokey Joe claims it was only a lucky shot. While on final approach, he encountered heavy enemy fire from guerrillas on the ground. After feeling a sudden shudder and hearing a horrific blast, Joe realized that he had taken a direct hit. Almost at once, alarms sounded and he realized one engine was engulfed in fire.

People who had witnessed the crash began calling him Smokey Joe. The nickname stuck with him wherever he ventured. He could still remember that harried crash landing. He had gotten out just before the damn thing exploded. Yes, Smokey Joe needed a career change.

Tempted to get into smuggling dope, he headed for Miami. Thank goodness he had let his conscience get the best of him and he opted for Chalk's Airlines. Shuttling passengers to and from the islands was a whole lot safer and carried a little more job security.

Today Smokey Joe could not resist sitting in the waters of Government Cut in Miami any longer. With his engines at fast idle, he visually checked each gauge. Yes, he thought, the old girl is nice and warm. Before the sun had even completely pierced the darkness and gloominess of the stormy night, Joe carefully pulled back the throttles. With a brief delay, the sound of the propellers began roaring to life, engulfing the seaplane in a mist of salt spray. Slowly he began his taxi.

The plane he was flying was almost an antique by today's standards. Built of highly polished aluminum by Grumman, the amphibious seaplane looked strangely out of place skimming across the channel usually inhabited by cruise ships.

Today he almost felt like he was in his glory days as he took to the air, carrying relief supplies and workers to the exclusive Cat Cay Island. With the high cost of Bahamian fuel, all of the plane's tanks and auxiliary tanks were fully loaded with fuel. This thought was reassuring considering that if their landing harbor was unusable due to hurricane debris, they would still have plenty of fuel to land some-where else.

In the early dim daylight, the sea still looked turbid as they crossed over the Gulf Stream. Without warning a strangely unfamiliar alarm began to sound. Checking his instruments, it registered as a distress signal from an EPIRB. Lowering his altitude Smokey Joe began to home in on the signal. At first all he could see was an oil slick. Soon after he began finding timber and other various ominous signs.

Following the line of floating footprints, Joe thought he

made out a life raft in the distance. Yes, mate, you still haven't lost them bloody good eyes, thought Joe, as he came across a bright orange life raft in the water below. Circling as slowly and as low as possible, he began making lazy circles. Joe was becoming disheartened. He had expected the excited waving of jubilant survivors; instead only a lifeless life raft loomed below.

"Coast Guard Station Miami, we've located a life raft, switch and answer on 22A", said Smokey Joe. "No sign of life, though, debris scattered for miles along an oil slick. Please advise. Must have been one hell of a night out here, mates."

"Chalk's 218 baker, please forward your position, we have a rescue helicopter airborne momentarily", responded the Coast Guard Miami group.

The small plane continued circling in the rising morning sun. Joe almost became hypnotic with each new circle. The sun's angle was just perfect so as to flash a blast of brilliance off the shiny airplane's strut with each rotation.

"Chalk's 218 baker, this is rescue 19 alpha, we have you on visual, any sign of life below you there?" came the welcomed sound of the chopper pilot.

"Negative, 19 alpha, been making one hell of a roar but no one seems to be home, mate," answered Joe.

The seas were still choppy as the helicopter approached and hovered, searching for signs of survivors.

Not wanting to risk sending in a rescue diver, they hovered just 50 feet over the raft. It was David who woke up first. The rotor wash off the already disturbed water gave David a feeling surreal in nature. Had he died? Was he dreaming? No, he was alive. This was help. He sat up in the raft.

"We have a survivor, we have a survivor, send in the divers, good job, 218 baker!" said the elated helicopter pilot.

The divers immediately dropped into the water. Their rescue basket quickly followed. In no time at all two jubilant survivors were headed for the mainland. Running low on fuel, the helicopter could not remain in the area and search for the others. Two planes were dispatched as daylight was now in full force.

Chalk's 218 baker continued to assist in the search. He stayed airborne until the bitter end. Like the old bush pilot he was, he stayed until he had burnt all his reserve fuel. It was with mixed feelings that he gave up searching and headed for Cat Cay.

Only a few minutes after sunrise, everyone remained inside Jim and Linda's home. With the stress of the night they had been through, everyone but Larry and Jim fell into a deep sleep. When there was just enough daylight outside, Jim slowly opened his front door and went out on the balcony. It had felt like the longest night he could remember. Thank God it was finally over. Looking around, Jim was stunned by what he witnessed.

His property looked as if a bomb had been detonated. With a few other exceptions, the only tree that looked unscathed was his favorite palm down by the water. Everything else was gone. His heart sank as he realized the work that laid ahead of him. The amazing thing, however, was his house. Except for their Ford Expedition and some water seepage that he could easily repair, he would not even have to file an insurance claim. State Farm would be happy for sure.

Together Larry and Jim walked as far as they could manage in both directions checking on neighbors. Thankfully, everyone but them had evacuated. Unfortunately, many pets that were left behind were not as lucky.

Not knowing exactly what to do next, Jim fired up his generator and made some coffee. With his cup in hand, he headed down to the water as he had done on so many other mornings. His dog, Skipper, had hidden out the storm in a closet. He ran out of the house and followed Jim down to the water. This morning was definitely different. He felt strange. The winds were now almost still. The sky above remained overcast but gave no indication of what horror the night had brought.

As he sat there, he began to think of his next move. It would be weeks before they had power again. The roads would not be passable for several days. Where should they start? With all that had gone on, he completely forgot about the Mystic Lady. He grimaced as he pictured her destroyed, in pieces scattered over several acres. He would like to head up the road and find out, but he could not find his vehicle. She also would have to wait.

Watching her husband, Linda shook her head. She decided to go down and comfort Jim. Walking up to him, she placed her hands on his shoulders and gently squeezed. "Don't worry, honey, it will be fine," she said, trying to reassure him.

Turning, he reached out, took her in his arms and smiled, then began to laugh. "Linda, I'm not sad. We made it! We've been to hell and back, and we are still standing," said Jim with a slight chuckle.

Reaching out and placing his hand on his weathered, old, trusty palm tree he said, "Besides, if we lost everything else, at least I have you and my favorite palm tree here." With his chair somewhere out in the bay, they sat down on the sea wall and sipped coffee together in the early morning light.

As if to let Jim and Linda know that things would mend, they watched as an early-morning bonefish was already at work tailing for food in the stirred-up sand beneath the shallow flat. Then looking up, Linda pointed out an osprey overhead. The bird flew down to some mangroves and flew off with some branches. It was already rebuilding its nest. Life would go on. Mother Nature had already begun the healing process.

EPILOGUE

As the day heated up, it became scorching hot. The humidity hung agonizingly thick in the air. Jim, Larry, John and Charlie worked to right as many trees as they could salvage. With the exception of a few news helicopters, they neither saw nor heard from anyone.

It was later that afternoon when Jim raised his head. In the distance he heard the distinct buzz of a small outboard motor. As it slowly came closer, Jim wondered who else had been crazy enough to also ride out the storm. Finally, a few more minutes later, a small inflatable red raft with a man in a Coast Guard uniform came through the mangroves. As the raft pulled up to the dock, Jim smiled a wide grin and said, "Henry, you made it!"

Waving, Henry tied up his boat and walked briskly over to them. "I sure did. How did you guys do?" asked Henry.

Raising his hands in the air, Jim said, "We did great. Except for our truck and the yard, we are in great shape. You want a cold drink, Henry?"

"I sure could use one. This heat is unbearable," said Henry. Going upstairs, Henry was sure glad to feel the cool air conditioning. He looked around in disbelief and said, "Man, when you called this place Fort Knox, you were not kidding. You even still have air conditioning?"

"Yeah, the place really surprised me, too. How does everything else in the Keys look?" asked Jim.

"There is nothing left. It's all gone. Looks like a nuke went off; everything was flattened. In some places, all that is left is bare coral rock where a house once stood. Contractors will be in hog heaven when they see the news tonight."

Sitting down and sipping a cold Diet Pepsi, Henry said, "Well, I have some bad news. One of your prisoners didn't make it. A wall supporting him gave way. I could not find him, and unless a miracle happened, he washed clear across Florida Bay."

A concerned look came over Charlie, who was listening in on the conversation. "Which guy bit it?" he asked.

"The scar-faced guy in the Cuban uniform was lost, the other guy is fine, just shook up as hell," answered Henry.

Smiling, Charlie looked up and said, "Hell, that's good news, Henry. We didn't know just what we were going to do with him anyway. Most likely we would have had to send him back where he would continue to plot ways to destroy us."

"I do know one thing that will make you feel proud. You are not going to believe where your boat ended up." Henry looked at everyone sitting there and said, "That damn boat of yours nearly wiped out my building. The tie-down job you did held her in place for as long it could. When she did let go, she made a beeline for your prisoner's cell. Her bow went straight in and knocked down the wall. You should see her, sitting dry-docked. Everyone else's boats kept on going out into the bay. I do believe that your boat can still float. Hull doesn't have a crack or any major problems. Even after going though my wall, there does not appear to be any major structural damage to the super structure. In a month you'll have her fixed up good as new and be fishing, I suppose."

Jim's eyebrows raised, and as he exhaled he looked like he was deflating. It was the tension leaving his body. It was not the best of news, but it could have been much worse.

"Well, I should be thankful, at least I have a boat. With that blow, every boat tied up in the mangroves sank for sure," said Jim.

"Henry, you mind giving Larry and me a lift? I sure would like to start the salvage process," said Jim.

"You bet, nothing going to happen around here for a few days," said Henry. Jim and Larry hopped aboard the red rubber boat and sputtered out into the bay. They had to see the Mystic Lady.

On the balcony, Charlie had an arm around Maria. Linda was leaning on the railing, smiling. For Charlie, this adventure had been God-sent. It was early, but he knew Maria and he would soon be inseparable. Maria was beaming. She almost glowed as she radiated her happiness of both standing on U.S. soil and finding Charlie.

Linda was tired, but she could not resist standing and watching as her favorite person on earth slowly disappeared in the little red boat. They had survived. It was not easy, but they made it. The cleanup would be long and hard. In a few years, though, it would be hard for anyone to remember just what a struggle took place here.

Although a fuel slick and large amount of wreckage were located, no one would ever find Capt. Phillip Debouis, still holding the wheel of the now-upside-down Beulah Pride, sitting unceremoniously at the bottom of the Gulf Stream.

Jean Matisse and Pierre Bonnard, although expelled from the wreckage, were never recovered.

Both Clayton Jones and David Jacques-Louis were released from Jackson Memorial Hospital the next day and were interviewed by news media across the country.